Shop

By the same author

BACK IN CHARGE

Shopping Around

Mariah Greene

LIBRIS

An *X Libris* Book

First published by X Libris in 1995

A CIP catalogue for this book
is available from the British Library

ISBN 0 7515 1459 4

Photoset in North Wales by
Derek Doyle & Associates, Mold, Clwyd
Printed and bound in Great Britain by
Clays Ltd, St Ives plc

X Libris
A Division of
Little, Brown and Company (UK)
Brettenham House
Lancaster Place
London WC2E 7EN

Chapter One

WITH A STEADY flicker, the dim night lights gave way
to the burning fluorescent of day. Lights designed to
be brighter than day itself. Display cabinets lit up,
instantly recognisable logos illuminated and goods
were displayed. Spot lights, strategically positioned,
would guide eyes in precise directions, towards
desirable commodities, things that had to be had.
Under a layer of total silence, the brightness changed.
The shop was stirring.

Karen Taylor sighed with contentment as the cock
entered her. She enjoyed sex first thing in the
morning, while most people were still sleeping. The
best way to wake up. He was pressing hard against
her, pushing himself in with a forceful enthusiasm. It
was the third time they had made love since entering
the bed the night before. Karen's favourite pattern.
Once when she got in. Once in the middle of the night.
Best of all, one final time in the morning. She raised
her knees higher, pulling the duvet so it came off his
shoulders, revealing his back, long and shapely. She
lifted her head and peered over his shoulders,
watching his back ripple and undulate, like a wave
spreading out from his rear-end and diminishing at his
shoulders.

Staff began to arrive. Some together. Some alone.
Some friends, some lovers and some enemies.
Through their own special entrance they filed, into the

infrastructure of the building. The brighter sparks shouted things cheerily at the less cheerful. A network of people too vast for everyone to want to know everyone else. Into the brightness of a new day, they immersed themselves.

He mumbled something against her ear, but Karen could not tell what it was. He obviously enjoyed it in the morning as well. Her pussy was warm and relaxed, comfortable and accommodating to the speed and depth of him inside of her as she gripped him tightly, both with her pussy and with her arms. His flesh was hot from the bed and his brow was developing the finest mist of morning sweat, like dew. A drop fell from him and landed on her collar bone, gathering in the cleft of skin and bone. Karen placed her hands on his sides, feeling the outer edge of his ribcage, so close to the surface and the skin so smooth and taut, his whole torso moving in her hands.

In the basement, a small army of good-looking men, all in their twenties, fussed around. They dressed and undressed mannequins, folded and re-folded garments that were displayed on tables and adjusted racks and racks of suits and jackets, discreetly tucking the price tags in. It was an expansive area hollowed out to a single level, the roof-supporting joists integrated into the decor of the room. The air-conditioning silently pumped an artificially cool atmosphere into the dungeon-like space, the only public entrance to which was a large and elaborate stone stairway, rough and granite-like. There was banter, in-jokes and gossip as the basement was preened and primped, the whole room dressed and ready for another day of being slowly undressed and tousled.

Her body was now fully awake to the passion it was experiencing. She had drifted through the light veil of sleep that had still shrouded her when she initiated sex and she was now fully cognisant, using all of her senses to their fullest potential. His weight was on her, compressing her into the mattress as each thrust pushed her against the sheet. In the early morning quiet of the room, what sounds there were became amplified. Her breathing, his breathing, the movement of the bed and the rub of the bed linen.

In the café, three of the four men who worked behind the counter were robed identically in white shirts, black trousers and a white apron, crisp and pressed. The espresso machine warmed up and the smell of coffee was in the air. Pastries were delivered from the store's bakery and set out in glass display cabinets. Fresh oranges, grapefruits, strawberries and cranberries were juiced and placed into large glass jugs while cups and saucers, plates and glasses were checked and stacked. Bar tops and the few small tables were given a final polish, condiments laid out in a precise fashion. In the back, the cook warmed the griddle and waited for the first rush to start.

Inside her, his cock was solid. It was a definite part of him that had planted itself inside a definite part of her. He had stopped thrusting for a moment and was resting his body against hers, his chest against her breasts, their hips still joined. As she lay, she felt him quiver and pulse his cock inside her and was conscious of its shape, the head so large and imploring when it had entered her the first time, a whole night ago. His pubic hair was weaved with her own and they were a mixture of sweat and juices, ready to pump on and bring them both to an elongated and painfully pleasurable orgasm.

On shelves of glass, the detailed and delicate china and glassware shimmered in the light and juddered almost imperceptibly from the movement of traffic outside and people around it. Cut crystal absorbed the light into its own pattern and refracted it with a brilliance and complexity that the lighting alone could never have achieved. In the aisles around the shelves, deep pile carpets in Wedgwood blue smoothed the path, carefully vacuumed each night. The whole area seemed fragile, easily shattered by even the slightest sudden movement. With the delicacy and care of archaeologists or museum curators, men and women polished the surfaces of glass.

His rhythm picking up where it had left off, Karen lent him encouragement by grabbing handfuls of his slinky behind and pulling him deep into her, squeezing his buttocks and raking them with her nails as she did so. She reached a hand over and down his crack, tickling his balls where they rested on her, making him yelp like a puppy. He was using his knees to lever himself and make his rush on her that much faster as his cock shafted her pussy with increasing speed, making Karen tingle and ache at the same time. She yearned for her orgasm but wanted to relish the sex some more, feel him over her and on her, in her and out of her. She wanted to hear him yell as he spilled into her, jerking and thrashing around on the bed, shattering the quiet of the dawn.

Down the centre of the department, suspended from a high point near the ceiling, ran a long and narrow catwalk. Mannequins were frozen in poses that both mimicked and mocked the supermodels who would ordinarily inhabit such a space. On the mannequins were the finest couture names, both new and old, clothes that were outrageous or conservative, bright or discreet. All, however, were expensive and lush, able to make even the plastic dummies appear casual and stylish, as though a moment from a Paris show had been frozen in time. The windows in the whole department were masked, as if by sunglasses, affording only a glimpse of the natural light outside.

Faster and faster he went into her and Karen could sense he was as close as she was, but not quite. She clung on to him, continuing to move in time with him, and readied herself.

The front doors opened and the first customers trickled through, regulars making their way to familiar destinations within the store.

The light of the new day filled Karen. As she came,

she was illuminated by it, the glow flowing through her and radiating from her. She was bathed in pleasure, burnishing her like the golden sun. Karen had coaxed herself from the dark of the night into the dawn of sex and now the sun rose gloriously in her, the steady and certain throb of her climax suspending her momentarily, freezing her in time before launching her. She exhaled heavily, the breath coming from deep inside her, and felt herself open out anew.

A new day had begun.

Chapter Two

KAREN TAYLOR ENTERED Sloane Square at ten-thirty, feeling and looking every inch the maverick. Her metallic Richard Tyler jacket practically screamed off of her, smothering the casual classic look of her Hermès trousers and Paul Smith shirt. She had been thirty for six months and relished every moment of it. She didn't know if she was in her prime, but she certainly felt better than she ever had and hoped the feeling would go on getting better and better.

She darted quickly over the zebra crossing, ignoring whatever the driver in the passing cab had said, and made her way to Hamiltons, the department store where she worked. Karen loved London, especially at this time of the day, when people had already started work and were into their routines. Sloane Square was always lively, a mix of cars and people frantically vying for any available space to occupy.

Switching her briefcase to her left hand, she ran a finger over each eyebrow, making herself feel in order. She was wearing her hair shorter than it had been for some time, and had applied mousse to make it fall in a gently tangled and tousled way that went just over her ears, while the fringe fell short of her eyebrows. The hair accentuated her look which was sensuous and soft. Her skin was smooth and even, nose slightly snubby, even cute, and her eyes were grey-blue, seeming to darken slightly at the rim of each iris.

Karen's face was the most striking thing about her and she had been told many times that she would not be out of place modelling cosmetics – the kind of advertisement where the face says it all. Somehow, she could never quite see herself shot through gauze and voiced-over by an out-of-work actress with a baritone and body hair. She was more proud of her body because she had worked at it, whereas her looks were a given. She pounded the metal at her health club and the result was a body pleasingly firm, displaying her most feminine aspects to their fullest – her long, shapely legs, tight stomach and well-formed rear. Her breasts were round and pert, barely needing the support of a bra.

People would have noticed her, whatever. She knew that. Even if she had not been as attractive, she would still have made herself noticed. That was the sort of woman she was.

From her favourite piece of the pavement, she eyed Hamiltons. It was a cross between a castle and the Bank of England. A white fortress with small turrets on either side, it took up most of one side of Sloane Square. Five floors and a basement, housing men's and women's clothing, perfumes, home wares, furniture, a bookshop and its own café. It was not the broadest mix but nor was it a paltry one. By virtue of being there in the first instance and because of its concerted attempts to win over customers, Hamiltons had survived.

In the years prior to her joining, the shop had gone through a slump and it had been rumoured for a time that it might be sold or even closed. When Karen heard via a friend that Hamiltons were looking for someone to manage promotions in the store, her interest was sparked. They were looking for someone who would run special campaigns to promote particular products or product lines, to pull people back into the shop. More than that, they wanted innovation and provocation, something that would give them a reputation

7

for flair, a shop not afraid to be daring. She knew she should have the job.

In a little more than three years, Hamiltons had shifted its axis from a slightly stuffy shop that most people thought sold haberdashery to old ladies on coach trips, to a store that was known for its daring and as a fun place to shop. For a whole month, she made everyone in the perfume department wear identical pairs of Revo sunglasses all day, on the instruction that they were not to answer any questions as to why they were wearing them. The store was written up in the evening newspapers and even got a mention on one of the London news programmes. More than just the sale of sunglasses jumped. Whatever Karen felt it took, she did. She loved her job and the freedom it gave her.

Today, a warm Wednesday in July, she was about to start the next phase of Hamiltons newest venture – a unisex skin scent. Hamiltons had entered into an arrangement with a medium-sized cosmetics company which was to be the perfect marriage of their production technology and Hamiltons' style and marketability. The marketing campaign was something of a double coup for Karen. Firstly, she had convinced Hamiltons owner Daniel Avendon that they should handle the concept side of the marketing themselves and, secondly, she had managed to secure Linda Cole, a cult photographer who shrewdly functioned on the borders of art and commerce, to do a shoot with Maxwell, the latest up-and-coming boy supermodel. Maxwell was perfect for it, an androgynous man-child, as ambiguous as the fragrance itself. Karen had been at college with Linda, so it was easy enough to arrange. With Linda attached to the project, getting Maxwell had been simple.

She looked up at the sky, smiling because she could see that the sun would be perfect by noon. With some careful negotiating and by taking Linda there, Karen had convinced everyone that the roof of Hamiltons would be the perfect place for the shoot. Linda had balked at first, but once she was up there, she too had agreed that it was a good location and that it would give the campaign continuity if all three publicity shots were done there.

As she entered the large brass door, the doorman, dressed impeccably in full livery, made a peace sign at her. She smiled and entered Hamiltons.

'Karen! Jesus, where've you been?'

It was David, her personal assistant. A nervous shiftiness and a shock of black curly hair were two of the three things that defined David for Karen. The other was that he was good at his job of looking after her and completely trustworthy. She could have told him what she had *really* been doing all morning, but David was beyond shock by now, so it would have been a wasted effort.

'Nice jacket,' he said, his concentration lapsing momentarily. He snapped back to attention. 'I've been calling you . . .'

'And leaving hang-ups on the machine. I knew it would be you. I suppose I can expect to find another five on my mobile messaging service?' She was even in her tone, not testy.

'Daniel's been looking for you. He wants to talk to you about this afternoon.'

'I thought he would,' she said. 'What did you say to him?'

'That everything would be fine.'

'And is everything fine?'

'No.' He looked at her and then at the floor.

'Did Linda arrive yet?' she asked, looking at him.

'She's been here since seven this morning, according to security. She's on the roof setting up. The bird handlers arrived an hour ago.'

'It sounds to me like everything's under control. Why so worried?'

'Daniel,' he said, using the word carefully.

Karen drew breath and looked around. The ground

9

floor housed the men's and women's fragrances as well as a gift shop. It had the noise and commotion of a train station at most times and now was little exception.

'Do we have a problem?' she asked.

'Yes.'

'David,' she said, touching his hand lightly, 'I'm going up to the café and I'll get us both a coffee, then you can relax and we can talk. First, I want to have a walk through the shop. See you up there in ten minutes.'

She walked away from him and his exasperated look, picking her way through the perfume girls, all yielding tester bottles as though they were Mace, and the aftershave boys all giving off the right degree of attitude. They all smiled at her, but she thought they would have smiled even if they were blindfolded and locked in a darkened room. It was their way. One day she would dress them all as rabbits who would stop the customers and ask if they could test the perfume on the humans.

While she stood on the escalator that took her to the second floor, she surveyed Hamiltons from the vantage point the height afforded. There was a buzz. Something she could never quite pin down or identify. It was like trying to see air. The shop was organic, a living thing that grew and had a life of its own that was over and above the simple sum of its parts. Daniel Avendon, the store's owner, liked to talk of it as a communal energy or Gestalt. To Karen it simply felt as though there was an air of expectation, the anticipation of someone arriving or having just arrived. Hamiltons' secret was making the customer feel like *they* were the one who had arrived. Each floor occupied several thousand square feet and the spaces were light and airy; chandeliers on the ground floor made it stately, while the clothes departments were fitted out in a more modern style. Each of the departments had its own decorative style and identity, but there was an overall theme of sumptuousness. Karen felt there was a wickedness in the air.

The smell of coffee from the third-floor café wafted through the air as the escalator neared its destination. She felt as though she were home, as though the shop were a part of her and she a part of it. Hamiltons had always been in the hands of the Avendon clan, but it had a tempestuous history. It had opened in the early Fifties and was carried along by a post-war optimism and the spending power of a class for whom it would have taken more than a war to spoil their shopping. In fact, Hamiltons was the outcome of a more specific war. A war between two families, the Avendons and the Foxtons.

Daniel Avendon's father Lawrence was the founder of Hamiltons and he had been in bitter competition with Dick Foxton, the owner of a nearby store. It was this rivalry that had kept Hamiltons sharp and sassy in the early days. According to Daniel, things turned sour when his mother Mary entered the fray and there was a battle between the two men over *her*. Karen had not properly established how the story ended, but in the space of a few years, Mary had married and divorced the both of them.

Her shoes bumped the top of the escalator and she turned her mind to more practical matters. She settled at the coffee bar and ordered two double espressos. David was there instantly – had probably been stalking her through the shop. He had a clipboard in his hand, on which would be written a schedule and a list of things to do. David's nose twitched and his cheek ticked nervously. He took it on himself to do all of Karen's worrying in addition to his own, all at the tender age of twenty-six.

'Tell me what's the matter,' she said, her eyes fixed on the waiter and his careful procedure for producing the coffee.

'It's the nudity. Daniel thinks we may be exposed.'

She laughed at his choice of words.

'*We* certainly won't be. Do you think he means the reputation of the shop or that the shoot itself may cause a problem?'

David shrugged and raised his eyebrows. She sipped at the coffee.

'Okay,' she said to herself. 'Where's Daniel now – he's not up there interfering, is he?'

David shook his head.

'When we've had coffee,' she continued, 'I'm going up on the roof to have a word with Linda. Give me about ten or fifteen minutes and then bring Daniel up. I'll introduce him.'

'Supposing he won't come up?'

'David, please. Daniel won't be able to resist. That's probably why he's kicking up a fuss. We should have let him meet Linda sooner. Trust me.'

She had drunk half of her coffee before she spoke again.

'Remember, David, only necessary people out there today. I don't want all the nellies from the dungeon up here ogling Maxwell.'

'It's taken care of. Hardly anyone knows we're doing it today and I've arranged for security to have a couple of people on the door to the roof.'

'Linda wants to shoot through lunch to make the most of the light. You did arrange for lunch to be sent?' she asked.

'They're sending it from here, around one-thirty.'

'Fine. I'd better get going. Take my case for me and head off Daniel for ten minutes,' she said, swallowing the last of the coffee and standing.

When she went out on to the roof, it was alive with activity. Linda was ordering two assistants to move things around and they scurried obediently while on a quiet corner of the roof, two middle-aged women tended to a dozen or so bird cages. A small plinth had been set up and flash units with umbrellas behind them were positioned at various heights. To one side was a large silver board that Karen had seen other photographers use to reflect the sun. Linda turned around and her face lit up when she saw Karen.

'Hi,' she said, rushing over and kissing Karen on the cheek. Linda was dressed in tight black ski pants with a similarly snug Lycra top over which was a looser black cotton vest. Her reddish blonde hair was pushed into a black baseball hat, her normally long earrings replaced by sleepers.

'I don't think I've ever seen you dressed for work before,' Karen said, stepping back and looking at her old college friend.

'If I look like a complete bitch,' Linda said, 'people will basically do as I tell them and then leave me alone. It works for me.'

'We might have a small hitch,' Karen said.

Linda's features remained neutral.

'My boss is getting a bit jumpy about the shoot. The nudity to be precise.'

'Karen, it's not going to work if he's wearing clothes. That's not the point of it, you know that. We've discussed it enough times.'

'I agree completely,' Karen said, nodding.

A tall wiry figure came through the door, went past them and made his way to the bird handlers.

'So what does this add up to, Karen?'

'Nothing, I hope. He'll be coming up here in a few minutes. He knows who you are and if you could just lay it on a bit, I'm sure things will be fine. He's a fan of your work.'

Karen looked over at the boy talking to the bird people. He was familiar. He bent to look into one of the cages and turned his face up to one of the women and said something. In her mind it clicked and Karen had to double-take, before whispering to Linda, 'Is that him?'

'Maxwell? Yes,' said Linda. 'He's absolutely fascinated by birds. Loves them. Let me have a quick word with him and then I'll introduce you.'

Karen watched as Linda leaned a hand on his

shoulder and bent to talk to him. He listened to her intently and nodded before straightening up. Linda smiled over at Karen and she took it as her cue.

'Max, this is Karen Taylor. She runs special promotions here. And she's an old friend of mine, so don't be rude to her.'

Karen was surprised by Linda's familiarity with him. It started to dawn on her why it may have been so easy to get him for the job.

'Nice to meet you, Karen,' he said, extending a hand.

His palm was wide and flat, the fingers long and spindly. The gesture of a handshake had an awkward formality to it. He was tall and skinny, dressed in jeans that were baggy on him but would have been tight on most other people. Long lank arms connected to narrow shoulders that barely supported his clothes. He wore a grey woollen polo shirt with a white T-shirt underneath.

Somewhere between sandy blond and red ginger, his hair was swept over his head in a centre parting which caused the two points of the fringe to rest just above his dark eyebrows. The brows contrasted with the hair enough to make Karen think it might have been dyed or, more likely, sun-bleached. The boy's jaw and cheekbone were almost at right angles and they reached a delicate point at a chin that protruded only slightly.

The general impression was an angular face that sat on a thin, white-skinned neck. He flicked his hair from his clear green eyes, revealing the famous tiny scar on the corner of the right one.

'I'm really looking forward to the pictures,' he said.

His tongue protruded slightly at the beginning of the sentence and he squinted and seemed to push all of his features forward as he spoke, to give the words more trajectory. The right side of his mouth lifted in a faint smile when he spoke, as though he were privately amused at something. Maxwell's mouth remained open, the tongue protruding through his lips

14

for a second before disappearing into his mouth. He pushed his bottom teeth on to his top lip. His nose was puggish and cute, his ears jugged. He's flirty, thought Karen.

'My, it's blowy up here,' a voice boomed from behind them.

It was Daniel Avendon. Dapper and a well-kept fifty-two, he would stand out of a crowd big enough to fill a football stadium as the most powerful and richest person there. It hasn't been ten minutes, Karen thought, annoyed at David who was nowhere to be seen.

'Daniel, this is my friend, the photographer Linda Cole.'

'Delighted,' he said. 'I saw some of your work at ICP Midtown in New York. Marvellous.'

Daniel was a stream of one-word adjectives.

'And is this the lad who'll be in the pictures?' he asked, turning imperiously to Maxwell and sounding like Mr Bumble from Oliver Twist.

'Yes, sir,' said Maxwell, holding out his hand. 'I'm Maxwell and I'm pleased to meet you.'

A wind picked up and Maxwell folded his arms, cradling an elbow in each hand and pulling his shoulders in frailly. The doves in the cages fluttered and the sound of their wings beating the air was syncopated against the backdrop of the wind and the strains of the London traffic. Maxwell turned round to look at the birds.

'Do you like birds?' Avendon asked Maxwell.

'Oh yes,' he said, the tongue protruding slightly. 'I love them. Look at this,' he finished, squatting eye-level with the cage. Avendon joined him and soon they were in a conversation.

Over their heads, Linda winked to Karen and they moved away.

'Max's father kept pigeons,' Linda said to Karen.

'How do you know so much about him?' she asked coyly.

'Karen, he's one of my favourite models. He's to die for in front of a camera. Wait and see.'

'If we get to see. If Daniel decides to get stubborn, we may not see anything,' Karen said.

'Surely he won't disappoint a famous photographer like me?' Linda said in an exaggerated tone. 'He's seen my work. At ICP. Midtown,' she left large and deliberate gaps between her words in an imitation of Daniel's grandeur. 'Just let Max turn on the charm.'

Karen looked at the two of them squatting and pointing at the birds, like father and son. The roof of Hamiltons gave a spectacular view of the London skyline from an angle and direction that few people got to see.

A few minutes later, Daniel Avendon walked past them.

'I look forward to seeing the photographs,' he said.

'Let's go to work,' said Linda. She turned to Karen. 'We'll be about an hour finishing the set-ups and stuff. Why don't you come back then?'

Karen could take a hint, and left the roof, filling the hour in her office, making calls and checking her mail.

When she returned, it looked like not much had changed, except that Maxwell now wore a white towelling robe, his chest just visible through the opening in it. Karen watched silently and after ten minutes of make-up and hair, Maxwell was ready. He sat in a chair, patiently waiting while Linda checked a few final things.

'Ready for you, Max,' she shouted.

With a complete lack of self-consciousness, as Karen would normally have understood the term, Maxwell stood and dropped his robe to the floor.

Naked, the skinny boy with pale skin was an absolute delight to look at. His hair dropped forward into his eyes and his large mouth was already poised, as if in anticipation of a kiss. His torso was slim and bony with hardly any muscle to see save for the faintest definition around his chest. The nipples were

16

red, encircled by the odd hair, and pert in the brisk air on the roof.

He stood on the plinth and Karen let her eyes run over him a number of times. His legs, like the rest of him, were fairly skinny and hairless. His cock was long but perfectly in proportion to him, his pubic hair a downy brown.

On the roof, Karen, the bird handlers, Max's stylist, Linda's two assistants and even Linda stood in silence. Despite the sunlight, it was windy on the roof. They were high enough not to be seen by too many windows, although a few people would be able to see. Karen had already cleared it with the local police in case they got any calls wondering what was happening on Hamiltons' roof.

The initial shot was the most involved and was being done first as it would be the hardest to get right or repeat. If they lost the light, they could do the other two another day.

'Max, let's practise a few times the way we said,' Linda instructed him.

He nodded and squatted down on the plinth, his hands on the floor in front of his feet and his chin resting on his knees. Karen looked at his hunched figure, balls dangling from beneath him despite the briskness of the wind. He held the squatting pose for a few seconds and then stood quickly, raising his arms to either side of him.

'Try and keep your head straighter towards the camera and not look up so much. Movement's good, though, nice and fluid,' Linda said to him.

Karen looked on. Several times he went through the movements, looking like a flower blooming as he went from a scrunched-up position to standing proud with his arms out to the side. After Linda's first instruction, his head came up level with the camera every time. Linda was taking some shots with a small instant camera and said things to her assistants who bustled around.

'Let's have the doves,' called Linda.

Maxwell squatted and held his position for twenty minutes. Karen looked at his lithe body and could see why he was one of the most successful male models in years. He had it. As with Hamiltons itself, it was not possible to locate precisely what *it* was, but Maxwell had it. She wanted to mother him, to be his sister, to be his friend and to be his lover who would fuck him senseless, all in one simple look. She felt envious of Linda if she really had captured him on more than just film.

Karen knew that the shot was a success. The doves had been positioned carefully all around his feet and then some behind him and in front of him, below the level of the plinth. Even more carefully, a dozen or so were placed on him, his shoulders, knees and head. At that point, he looked absurd, like Nelson on top of the column, but when he stood on Linda's cue, his movement was one of sheer liquid flexibility and Karen could see in her mind a photograph of Maxwell bursting forth from a sea of doves, his hands held out by his sides, face etching itself into the camera and the grain of the London skyline behind him. Linda's cameras had been clicking frantically and Karen looked forward to going through the contact sheets with her.

The rest of the afternoon slipped by. While the bird handlers recovered the doves, Linda took Maxwell off to one of the turrets where they would do a shot not involving birds. His stylist fussed over him, fixing his hair and spraying it. Linda said something to the stylist and she went off to get something. He slipped his robe back on and they talked to each other. Karen observed, not wanting to get too much in the way of Linda but fascinated to see if she could discern any sort of relationship between them.

She suddenly became aware that David was by her side, cradling his clipboard.

'How's it going?' he asked her.

'Fine,' she responded, still looking at Linda and Maxwell.

'Daniel's happy then?'

'Very, as he would say. Any calls for me?'

'A few, but nothing I couldn't handle. You just concentrate on up here,' he said to her, surveying the ever present clipboard. Some people in the shop laughed at his clipboard, Karen knew, but she did not tell David.

'He's quite stunning, isn't he?' David remarked.

Karen turned to look at David, surprised.

'He must be to rouse your interest,' she said, a friendly mocking in her tone.

'You know what I mean.'

'I do. I do,' she said, realising that she was practically sighing. David left her to it.

Like a small and perfectly pretty gargoyle, Maxwell sat on the turret wall and Linda shot him from behind, looking out on London. He wore a pair of angel's wings held tightly on to him by leather straps. His head was hung slightly and the hair pushed forward and held by whatever industrial-strength concoction the stylist had recently applied.

'I think I'll call this one "Forlorn Angel",' Linda confided to Karen during a break.

'When do we get to choose which pictures are best?' Karen said gleefully, wondering if it were moral to enjoy her work so much.

'Monday or Tuesday next week. I'll call you.'

'Are you getting enough good stuff?' Karen asked.

'Plenty. We'll have trouble choosing. I always do with him.'

Maxwell was back where he was happiest for the last shot, on a plinth. Again he was naked except for a large leather gauntlet covering his right hand and on which was perched a peregrine falcon. Instead of the bird, it was Maxwell who wore a leather hood. Karen looked on as the afternoon light faded, studying his naked body, drinking every inch of it in, her eyes soaking him up like the film in Linda's camera. His image made her feel restless, desire sparking in her.

She pulled her mobile phone out and dialled Hamiltons' switchboard. After a few moments, she was put through.

Chapter Three

KAREN TOOK THE lift up to her sixth-floor apartment. Most days she would walk, but today she was tired. It had been a successful day and with most of it spent looking at a nude boy supermodel, it had been a sexy one too. She was ready to unwind. While the plush lift carried her, she shook off the silver jacket and hung it over her shoulder. Casually she sauntered along the hallway to her door, opened it and entered.

Keeping a flat on Sloane Street, midway between Knightsbridge and Sloane Square, was a minor indulgence on Karen's part, but she loved the place and its location. She would not have considered herself to have come from money, certainly not in the scale of the Daniel Avendons of the world, but her family were comfortable and the flat was the only thing for which she partly relied on them. She could walk to Hamiltons in just over five minutes and, in the other direction, she could reach Harvey Nichols and Harrods in the same amount of time. In terms of her universe, she felt her apartment placed her very much at the centre of it.

The flat itself consisted of five rooms on one level; living room, dining room, a study and two bedrooms. As was common for the area, the ceilings were high and the rooms large and square. Mostly furnished when she moved in, it was decorated in neutral shades of white, green and blue throughout. In her living room she had two identical black leather sofas that were overstuffed and oversized, like hotel furniture. A small shelf of books and a few racks of compact discs were her main source of entertainment, the TV large and largely unwatched in a corner. The living and dining area both had bird's eye maple floors with expensive rugs and the other rooms were lushly carpeted.

Karen went to the bedroom and kicked off her shoes, throwing the jacket on to the bed at the same time. She removed the bracelet that went with the outfit and placed it on the teak dressing table along with her earrings. She sat and looked at herself in the mirror briefly, picking up the brush and running it through her hair several times. Over the shoulder of her reflection, the bed loomed large and low, the mattress set on a plinth that was about six inches wider than the mattress itself. The sheets and covers were pure linen and she looked forward to sinking between them. Standing, she wriggled out of her tights and put them into her wicker laundry basket.

In the kitchen, she fished a bottle of mineral water from the fridge, the rubberised tiles of the floor warm on her bare feet. The units were a light ash and the work surfaces marbled. It reminded her of a display kitchen she had seen in the window of Heals.

In the living room she put a compact disc into the machine and sank into one of the sofas, drinking her water from the bottle and feeling cradled by the triumph of mood-lighting the strategically placed lamps always managed to achieve. When the buzzer rang, she almost did not want to get up. Then she thought of the cool and crisp linen sheets that awaited her in the bedroom.

'Hello,' she said on the entry phone.

'It's me,' his voice came back, crackled but confident.

She smiled and pushed the button on the wall unit.

'Very nice,' she said, pulling on his waistcoat as he

stood in the doorway.

'It's Dries Van Noten,' he said.

'All of it? The whole outfit is Dries? Surely not?'

'No, the shirt's Comme des Garçons.'

'And the trousers, let me guess,' she said, tugging at one of the pockets, 'are Armani?'

'Wrong,' he said, deepening his voice at the end of the word. 'They're Rykeil Homme. And my boxers are . . .'

'Shush,' she said, putting a finger to his mouth, 'I'll find that out soon enough.'

She studied him. Richard Fraser was twenty-five and would have looked more comfortable modelling most of the clothes he sold for Hamiltons. He had been working in the menswear basement for seven months and Karen had spotted him early on. She had assumed that, like most of the men down there in what the women at Hamiltons referred to as The Dungeon, Richard would be a boy who liked boys. The discovery that he was not sent a minor ripple of excitement through many women at Hamiltons, giving Richard some instant celebrity status and a rarity value if nothing else.

He was model-good-looking, she thought to herself. His mane of hair, mid-brown and not light enough for him to be considered blond, was pushed back over his head in a way that was meant to imply a careless hand had ploughed a rough furrow into it. In truth, Karen knew that many hours of grooming and chemical additives had gone into giving it the fake-casual look. This calculated devil-may-care coiffure gave him the demeanour of a good boy who wanted to turn bad. In truth, his features were too angelic for that and he was sensible enough to realise it, dressing himself carefully in a relaxed way. To Karen he was the product of a thousand labels.

The post-choir boy, post-public schoolboy face made Karen want to grab for him almost continually. His eyes were a quiet blue-grey and his mouth delicate and formed from well proportioned lips. The jaw and cheekbones had the angles that would hurtle aerodynamically down a catwalk if required, and she had seen him mould his features into a smoulder on more than one occasion, his rich golden colouring promising hot days in the sun and hotter nights in bed.

'So are you going to tell me why you were such a bitch to me today?' he said to her over his shoulder as they went to the living room.

She ignored him and went to the fridge to get another water for herself and one for him.

'It was a difficult time,' she said, returning. 'We were in the middle of the photo shoot and I was down in my office for a quick break and to return a few calls. Plus, Alan Saxton was there breathing down my neck. I can't just stop and chat away like some bimbo. I'll look like one of the Saturday girls, gabbing away to her friend about the weekend while she's serving someone.'

'What did he want anyway? Is the old fart sniffing around you?'

'Richard, please. He's old enough to be my, well your, father. I'm not in that market. He was checking on one of the items on the budget for the underwear promotion we're doing in the basement.'

'I'm sorry. I know it's hard. Big power woman and the humble shop boy. We're like a fairy-tale cartoon,' he smiled.

'You are so cheeky, sometimes.'

She went and sat next to him on the sofa. In profile, his features were sculpted and he was very pretty, his lips pouting away from the solid line of his jaw. She explored the material on the waistcoat's shoulder with her hands and then on up through his hair.

'Careful!' he said to her as she moved his hair about in her fingers.

'Don't be so vain,' she said to him, cupping the back of his head in her hand and pulling him towards her so she could kiss him. She enjoyed homing in on his even

24

complexion, the skin unblemished and soft, ready for her caress. She wanted to blow on it gently and watch it twitch under her breath.

Karen leaned up on the sofa and pushed him back into it as they kissed, using his shoulders for support, the linen of his waistcoat delicate under her fingers and reminiscent of the bed sheets she had eyed so longingly before Richard arrived. Soon, she was sitting astride him and she kissed him in long and deep repetition, tasting him and smelling the waft of his aftershave, still sweet in the early evening heat. Her skirt had ridden up to reveal the tops of her thighs, bare without her tights, and his hands rubbed them, leaving goose bumps in their wake.

Sitting back and resting her weight on Richard's legs, his cock pushing at her behind, she took the waistcoat off him, and he leaned forward to allow her to lift it from his back and on over his head like a jumper. It was the first small stage towards nudity and she relished the journey. She enjoyed removing, one by one, Richard's collection of labels, leaving him bare before her with only his own label to show. Devoid of his clothes, of the symbols and tag and mark of another, he had never disappointed her so far. His body was supple, with only a faint tendency towards muscularity, mostly around his chest and stomach muscles. Working out at the gym, Karen could appreciate a good body when she saw one. At that moment, she wanted more than anything to see one. His.

When the buttons at the front of his shirt were undone to the waistband of his trousers, she tugged it open as though he were Superman rushing towards a phone box. She lifted and moulded his chest muscles in her hands, her thumbs flicking at the small hard nipples which had a trace of dark hair around them. The rest of his torso was hairless apart from the line of hair that began under his navel and which she knew journeyed down to his mat of pubic hair but was at that moment stopped abruptly by his trouser line.

25

Karen leaned closer to him and kissed him again, darting her tongue out and letting it catch the underside of his top lip to feel the sharpness of his teeth. Between her legs her pussy was coming to life and she shifted herself on him to calm its stirring. She held each of his hands in turn while she undid the cuff and gauntlet buttons on the white cotton shirt and then that too, in the same way as the waistcoat, came off. His body was a gentle V shape from shoulder to waistline, his navel protruding a quarter of an inch and the muscles of his stomach a tight palette of six even sections.

Concentrating fully and completely on her task at hand, she dropped to her knees on the floor and worked on his belt, slithering it slowly through the loops on his trousers, watching it unfurl from around him. The button at the top of his trousers came undone easily and she unzipped his fly, splaying it open at the top.

'Ah,' she said, 'so the underwear was Armani. I thought there would be some somewhere.'

He grinned at her and shifted restlessly on the sofa.

Removing his shoes and socks, amazed at how the gold of his skin extended to every extremity, she reached up and pulled off his trousers. He was left on the sofa in only a pair of white boxer shorts with a large white label on the front of the waistband like real boxer's shorts. The underwear was stark and white against the black leather on the sofa and the golden glow of his skin.

She used his hips for support and kissed at his chest, concentrating on one nipple at a time, the flesh pink and solid in her lips. She stood up, towering over him as he sat spread on the sofa. In a slow and confident manner, Karen removed all of her clothing. Shirt, the Hermès trousers, bra and pants, all came way from her body in a swift and practised routine which she knew would excite him. It excited her. She lifted her breasts and stretched her back, feeling herself loosen and spring free in the twilight breeze of her living room while Richard looked on. For a few seconds she toyed at her pussy, dipping her finger to a shallow depth, parting the lips slightly and nudging her clitoris.

Again she kneeled and this time she stroked him through his underwear. The shorts were pulled high, accentuating the length of his legs, his thighs taut and the flesh so inviting. Up the side of his leg she ran her hands, and when they found the white cotton of the boxers, she pressed into his flesh, feeling the density of his body. She pushed her fingers into the leg of the boxer shorts and felt the side of his buttock, raking her nails over the flesh. The elastic of the waistband stretched under her fingers when she gripped it at either side, ready to slip it down over his long legs, pausing briefly to allow him to remove his cock. She tugged at the shorts.

His underwear removed, she studied his cock intently. As she moved closer, she felt its heat rise to her face and caught the light manly musk in her nostrils. His left ball hung lower than the right and was fuller in his sac, which she reached out and compressed with her hand, causing him to sigh. The skin of his scrotum looked like a well worn material and was lightly covered in hair with a thin wrinkle of flesh running up its centre, almost as though it were dissecting a line which his balls hung either side of. Where the base of his cock began, the skin around his balls was heavily wrinkled and the lines shifted as his growing ardour caused the testicles to sway of their own accord. The sac seemed to tighten and the balls draw into him.

The beginnings of an erection had lengthened his cock as she watched it, like a timelapse camera showing the growth of a flower over a period of months. The tumescence had pulled back his foreskin and revealed the red phallus which was seeping a clear fluid in the smallest drop, an outward sign of his inner desire. The skin on the shaft of his cock was darker than the rest of him, not as golden, and criss-crossed with a map of blue veins. As he stiffened, the cushion his skin gave to the veins thinned and they came to the surface, as if the skin were translucent.

Karen held the shaft and drew Richard's foreskin back over the head of his cock, watching the loose skin gather under the top of his glans, wrinkling in the same pattern as his ball sac. The phallus was wide at the glans and rounded at the tip in a way that would make the penetration into her so pleasurable as it pushed at her lips and then opened her vagina and found its way into her.

But she did not want that right there and then, she realised. There would be time for that. First, she wanted to taste him and to swallow him and to have him do the same to her. She held his hands and pulled him to the floor, pushing him over on to his back, his hair falling loosely about him.

Karen sat astride his chest, a knee under each of his armpits. She thrust her hips at him, displaying her pussy, then pulled away again. He started to rub the fronts of her thighs but she slapped his hand away.

'I can do that myself,' she said, leaning forward and lowering herself into his face before he could say anything.

Richard's whole mouth worked on her, his tongue driving into her, wet and hot at the opening of her vagina. Her juices ran and he took them eagerly, his face muscles contracting and relaxing while he tongued her. Bit by bit, the muscles between her legs loosened and she became elastic and slick, relishing the noises she heard him make on her, the feel of his nose grazing her pubic hair.

With the intensity and speed of a lash, his tongue thrashed her clitoris, which was inflated and heaving from its own fullness. Her head was in a spin, heat rising around her face, and she felt flushed with emotion as he toyed with her. She was leaning over and resting her hands on the floor, knees open wide and breasts dangling free and weighty, two pendulous mounds. His hands were all over her lower back and behind, kneading and pressing the flesh, occasionally parting the cheeks; sometimes a finger ran under and touched the base of her pussy.

She wrenched herself from him before it was too late, not wanting to let herself spill into orgasm just yet. She wanted him to carry on feeding from her pussy, but she wanted to taste him too, to feed from him. Karen got off him and rolled him over on to his side. She lay facing him on her side also, but with her head in his crotch.

Immediately, he was at her again, barely pausing for breath. She felt his head move closer and he shuffled around on the living room rug, making himself comfortable. One side of his face rested on her leg and he hitched her other leg over the side of his head, so that he was completely buried in her. She waited and enjoyed the feeling he was giving her before turning her attention to him.

The cock which she had examined with such interest earlier had grown and pumped itself until it was almost unrecognisable. Seen from this angle, Richard *was* the good boy turned bad as his flaming cock hung inches from her face, pressing towards her. She followed the line from his balls under to the cheeks of his behind, the skin darker and less gold, a secret place exposed to her close examination. She wondered how many women had seen him this way, such a basic part of him, writhing and moving.

Karen pulled on his thigh and used it as a pillow. She took his cock and quickly put it in her mouth, not lingering, but eager to get the taste and heat of him in her mouth. Their sixty-nine position meant that his cock was upside down, and she savoured the inversion, sensing the difference as his glans was in the roof of her mouth and the ridge of his phallus against her tongue. It was tart, the small warm emission from the head of his penis, and Karen let it sit

29

on her tongue, the bitterness giving way as his flavour was diluted by her mouth. She was assimilating him into herself. The rest of his shaft filled her mouth with both its size and its heat, and she forced her lips wide apart to insert as much of him into her mouth as she could.

The feel of him in there was delightful, the skin of his shaft supple against the curve and contour of her mouth, the head of his cock rubbing against her. She closed her mouth and sucked hard, as though on a straw, but instead if drawing in air, it was his member which she closed around tightly and gulped further into her mouth. The shape of it was pronounced, the skin on the inside of Karen's cheeks drawing through her teeth and touching the side of Richard's shaft.

Down below, in her pussy, she was assailed by him and his tongue which felt as though it must have been stretching painfully to its root to burrow into her in the way it was at that moment. Her legs trembled from their position and from her passion and she wanted to come but also wanted him to come. She set to work on his cock in earnest.

It was a question of finding the right timbre with him, of moving in a way that was just right or at least close enough. He was unable to give her any verbal direction as his face was attached firmly to her crotch, so she made what she thought would be the most excruciating and exciting movements with her mouth and tongue. It seemed to be working, she thought, as he wriggled and began to pump with his groin. His legs were long and muscular and Karen enjoyed running her hands over the back of his thighs, the hairs tickling her palm.

She took the base of his cock with one hand and used the other to hold on his hips. She bobbed and ducked her head, his cock making her lips tingle. It was coated in her spittle, shining as the light from the lamps caught him as though he were lit for a take in a movie. As she manipulated him with her mouth, her abrasions against him fell into time with her breathing and she opened her mouth to allow some air in. Momentarily, she took him from her mouth and masturbated him, enjoying the sight of just his cock, knowing he was up there somewhere, feeling him inside her, his tongue toiling on her clitoris.

Karen closed her eyes and her mouth practically fell back on to his cock as she sucked wildly. She felt her orgasm, the one she had delayed earlier, come back to haunt her like the ghost of an old friend. It murmured deep within her, communicating a deep and arcane feeling that spilled into her consciousness and made her shut her eyes even tighter and give out small squealing sounds which were blocked by Richard's cock. She straightened her back, almost slipping her pussy away from his face and he followed her movement, quickly clamping himself back on to her.

In order to cry out, to let the fury of her passion loose in the room, she took his cock from her mouth and worked on it with her hand, partly to stimulate him and mostly to hold on to something, anything, for fear that she would slip away into her orgasm and be swallowed by it. She clung to him and came. It was like ice melting from heat in one sudden and powerful blast, as if from a furnace. She was a combination of hot and cold, the two sensations working in her and playing off each other, resulting only in ecstasy.

Her body contorted and bucked, but all the time Richard held her and kept his face in her, his tongue less insistent, merely fooling with her in a way that prolonged the giddy peak she had just reached and was enjoying the fall away from. She still held him in her hand and was sheathing him back and forth more from the movement of her whole body than from her arm. It had become like a beacon for her, the one thing she was clinging on to and she had almost forgotten her real purpose for grabbing him in the way she did.

He cried out in desperation and then in sudden and definite resignation. Her eyes were still closed and she was dizzy and in a dream-like state halfway between the worlds of awake and asleep. The first heavy drop of his come caught her on her right cheek and the shock of it made her open her eyes. She saw the eye in the head of his penis open and push forth another spurt of thick white semen. It landed on her chin and its distinctive odour rose to her nostrils. When the next jet sprang from him, she had firm hold of him and it landed on her tongue, splashing up onto the roof of her mouth. She could tell he was watching her now, looking down to see what she was doing. He ejaculated several more times and she moved him around, splashing her face with him.

They held on to each other, still in their inverted position, wanting to simply cling on to flesh and feel its warmth and texture, the pulse of life through it.

And they hadn't even made it into the linen of her bed.

Yet.

Chapter Four

'*HERE'S TO ANOTHER* success,' said Alan Saxton, gently clinking his large brandy glass against Karen's.

'How many times have we toasted it now?' She smiled. 'From the water, the wine, the champagne, of course, but even the coffee and now the brandy. Let's wait until we see the pictures.'

'I wish we could have toasted it yesterday,' he said, 'on the day it happened. While it was still hot off the presses, as it were.'

'I know. I'm sorry, Alan. I had a family thing to do that had been planned for ages. You know what families are like, they set things up months in advance, you say yes, completely forget about it and then suddenly realise it clashes horribly with something.' She felt she had gone on for too long, overcompensating her lie to the point where it was obvious. She sat and felt as if there were a sign around her neck saying 'I was with Richard last night.'

'I understand. I don't expect either of us to be at the call of the other,' he answered.

They had shared a long and relaxed meal together. Alan had brought her some flowers, ordered champagne and chatted easily with her. That simple. What Karen would normally have called the full works. With Alan, though, he was not trying to impress her. She knew this was how he would be with anyone he was attracted to. Like the restaurant itself, he was smooth, efficient and comfortable. Another part of him was too sheltered and sweet to try any bravado.

An inch over six feet and a year under fifty, Alan Saxton headed the finance division of Hamiltons. He oversaw all the shop's financial affairs and his influence was wide. He was a knowledgable and powerful man and he conveyed it in his physical presence and in the quiet but confident manner of his speech. Outside of Daniel Avendon, he knew more about Hamiltons than anyone.

Karen would not have said fifty if she was asked how old she thought Alan was. He was not young, but nor did he look his age. His shoulders were broad and she had been surprised at how well his body was kept. His hair was a wave of black for at least eighty per cent and the rest was grey in streaks that made him distinguished without looking stuffy. Karen thought he was sexy and forceful in a cabinet-minister sort of way. He was mature and had a charisma that could fill a room, in a sedate fashion, like a soft glow. She had noticed him many times when she first started work at Hamiltons but never dreamed she would end up sitting across the table from him at a romantic dinner for two.

'I think its nice to toast whenever possible,' Alan continued, oblivious to her train of thought. 'You so rarely get a chance to these days. I prefer intimate toasts between two people, not like wedding rabble.'

He looked at her as he spoke.

She reached and lighted her hand on his, where it cradled the brandy glass. His fingers were full and powerful. She brushed his knuckles lightly with her fingertips and looked at his hand. With her eyes she trailed up his arm and came to rest on his face. He was still looking at her, but shifting his gaze slightly, as though the intimacy was making him jittery. She gently removed her hand.

'What's next for you?' he asked.

'Oh, there's the sports promotion. They want to run

it in the Autumn to try and boost sales. It would be a change to do something that had more of a life expectancy. The campaigns come and go,' she said.

'I thought you would enjoy that. It seems in keeping with you.' He smiled.

'An unfocused flirt?' she chided him.

'Of course not. Just that you don't seem the sort of person who would want to be tied down to a single thing.'

'It depends on the thing. And the underwear promotion before the Autumn sports. A bit of a rush, but I'll slot it in.'

'How will you promote underwear? It seems a bit of a need-it-or-you-don't product to me.'

'Do you mean don't need as in don't wear any?'

He reddened almost imperceptibly, the skin around his mouth quivering slightly.

'No. No, I meant, you either have enough or you don't.'

'I bet you've never once gone anywhere without underwear, have you, Alan?' she asked him.

'Probably not since I was a small lad.'

'I'll sort you out some nice boxer shorts from the promotion, promise,' she said, recalling that on their two previous encounters, he had been in Y-fronts.

'Thank you – no,' he said to her in an exaggerated way.

He gave off the soft glow again. It was the same when he had first asked her out, six weeks earlier. He had met her in a corridor. She thought they had bumped into each other casually, but on reflection she realised he must have planned it. He was nervous and shifted his expensive shoes around on the polished floor.

Instantly, from the look on his face, she knew that he was going to ask her out. He acted like a schoolboy, mumbling – and at the same time he was asking her out, he was telling her she probably wasn't interested. In fact, he *was* just a schoolboy, she thought. Karen, like most people at Hamiltons, had heard he was recently separated from his wife Margaret and that it had been painful. They had been together since they were at university. Karen knew she was most likely the first woman he had asked out since then, so his chances to practise his chat-up skills would have been limited. She was both flattered and interested enough to say yes.

She had only one regret and that was not telling Richard about it and, similarly, not telling Alan about Richard. If they had both worked somewhere other than with her at Hamiltons, she would have, but something about the situation felt difficult, as though she was caught in a crossfire of feelings for the two of them and from the two of them. Predictably, as time rolled on, it had become hard to the point of impossible to tell one about the other.

For the first three weeks, they saw each other once a week. Very proper with minimal physical contact, apart from the occasional half-accidental brush and an obligatory goodnight peck. She was careful to keep the subject of his wife out of the conversation. He did not mention her very often and did not, on the surface at least, seem terribly upset. Karen sensed, however, that deeper in him something was working itself through and she was not sure how it would make itself known.

In the fourth week and after as many dates, they went to bed together. He was careful and considerate, certainly not as reserved as he was in public, but not an animal. The power that was there in his everyday life, bristling just below the surface, remained there also when they were in bed together. She wondered if she could coax him out of himself. She puzzled as to what might be a hot button for him, what would turn him on. He was nice to her, she found him attractive and she found the idea of pushing down his sexual barriers a challenge. So, six weeks later, as she sat in an expensive restaurant in Fulham, she found herself, gently and unwisely, falling for him.

There wasn't even just the single reason of Richard, telling her why she should not get involved. On the contrary, there were a few other good reasons. He was older. He was still married. He worked in the same place as her. They had different friends and interests. The list rolled through her mind like the credits for *War and Peace*. Still, as she watched Alan settle the bill and then look up at her with an expectant lift of the eyebrows, she felt herself free-fall a fraction further. She checked herself mentally, wondering if rather than falling for him, it was her job to let him down. Gently and soon. Now, perhaps?

'Will we go back to my house?' he asked her.

'I'd love to,' she said.

Alan's house was, like the restaurant, also in Fulham. In the expensive part, naturally. Two storeys high and a basement down below, he and Margaret had occupied it all. Karen wondered how the two of them had managed to fill out its expanse. Padding through it on his own must be hard, she thought.

Karen felt the buzz of the wine and champagne. She had not drunk too much but just enough had been consumed to give her the feeling that she blended perfectly with everything around her. It heightened her senses of touch, taste and smell but slowed her reactions just enough to enable the amplified feelings to linger in her. She was relaxed and she felt safe.

She sat on the sofa in the drawing room. It was just after eleven-thirty and the house was quiet. Karen could sense its size around her. He came back from hanging his coat and stood in front of her. She looked up at him and he held his hands out to her. She looked quickly at his trousers and saw they were pushing out at the front. He moved his fingers slightly in front of her face, giving a sense of urgency to his need, his desire for her to take his hands. She reached out and put her hands in his. He closed his palms and pulled her up firmly from the sofa.

As she reached her feet, so their mouths met in a kiss. He was taller than her by several inches and she tiptoed to give herself added height. In turn, he craned his neck down to make contact easier. Their mouths moved over each other, looking for a pattern that worked. The rhythm of their kiss was syncopated and they both gasped for breath after a few moments.

'That was nice,' she said to him.

'Very,' he replied, raising his eyebrows, eyes widening as he did so.

'Do you want to take me to bed, Alan?'

He nodded.

She touched the woollen material that covered his crotch, finding the shape of his cock and pushing to one side. It was firm. Gently she played her fingers over the material of his trousers, in much the same way as she had done to his fingers in the restaurant earlier. He gave an urgent gasp. Karen stepped an inch closer to him, coming fully into his space. She felt overpowered by it. The small step she had taken, just an inch, perhaps less, changed all of her feelings. His strong arms encircled her and she felt drenched by his presence, any previous doubts eradicated.

'Take me to bed, please,' she said.

What had a few moments earlier been a question now became a plea which she delivered hoarsely. He led her by the hand.

They fell on to the bed together, still fully clothed. As they kissed, she kicked off her shoes. Karen was wearing one of her favourite outfits, a suit by Romeo Gigli in a heavy brown stripe. Now Alan was pushing the high single-breasted jacket off her shoulders. He knelt up on the bed and lifted her shoulders, pushing the jacket further down her back. It was crumpled under her and she frantically wriggled her arms free as his hands quickly undid the belt on her trousers. These were round her ankles and off before she had time to move her legs. With hardly a moment for titillation, Alan removed her stockings and suspender belt. Karen pulled the jacket out from under her and discarded it, not bothering to look where it landed.

On the large double bed, Karen lay wearing only her knickers, blouse and bra. She felt half undone. Alan did not remove any of his own clothes. She looked at him as he leaned over her and kissed her. His eyes were alight and his hair fell forward. The calm exterior, the brooding power, had been replaced by a fervour. She relaxed as he swiftly unbuttoned her blouse. Her body wanted his touch. So far he had been undressing her with a ruthless speed but he had not touched her skin. She wanted him to caress her and touch her breasts. To rub his hand against the softness of her stomach and down on into the soft mound between her legs.

In seconds, she was nude. He was up on his knees, kneeling over her naked form. He bent and kissed her. As he did, she felt his hand between her breasts, the side of his little finger between the cleft. Her skin was warm and she felt a trace of moisture. A thumb circled under one of her breasts and came to its apex, pressing her nipple, pushing it back into her. He allowed it to pop out again and then she felt him circle its tip with his thumb. Her nipple stood proud and under his touch it became for a moment the most sensitive part of her body. Even as he kissed her and began to probe her mouth with his tongue, her nipple sang out.

When he broke the connection of the kiss, Karen leaned up on her elbows and brought her knees up, feet sliding up the bed as she did so. She dropped her knees wide, displaying herself to him. She saw his eyes run from the top to the bottom of her tight body. As they tracked over her body time and again, his look took on the feeling of a touch and she shuddered under it. Over her face, down her neck and on to her chest, where her breasts hung weightily, the heavy and delicious feeling of sex. The same feeling of sex ran along her taut stomach, the navel, and down into the cavern she had created with the position of her legs. Her juices drizzled slowly and she felt them lubricate the slit of her pussy. She was gripped by the temptation to rub herself with her own hands, but she resisted.

She looked at Alan. His cock seemed to fill the whole front of his trousers. Karen wanted to spring him free and massage him. Hold him in her hand and in her mouth. And then inside of herself, moving the both of them closer towards release.

He touched her pussy and she closed her eyes slowly, placing herself in a white-grey world. She had blocked her vision and was going to use her pussy as the only point of focus. His finger, the middle one, made a small line up and down her pussy lips. It went up towards her clitoris, just near enough to give her a shudder.

He introduced it into her quickly and determinedly and she cried out. She was thrown into tumult by the hard and harsh invasion and she relished it. Her juices helped smooth its way as she writhed on his finger, letting it play inside her and push its way deeper. His sturdy digit was in her to the second knuckle and his thumb was resting near her clitoris, as though it was waiting for her to go to him. She flicked her head about and heard the sound her movements made against the bedclothes, noises that were absorbed by the insulation of the whole house. Again she felt the size of the house looming large around her and how small she was inside of it.

The juices flowed from her as she became more pliant and she wondered where it was all coming from. She was overrun by him and his invasion into the narrow passage between her legs. He overpowered her as he deliberately swivelled his finger inside her, causing her to try and move with it. Its rhythm was so different from that which she would have used on herself that it increased the intensity of the experience. That and the fact that at that moment she found Alan himself to be so different from how she knew him. The reserve had gone. It had given way to an energy that both enthralled and frightened her. She was afraid she would lose herself in him even though she desperately wanted to.

He stopped just when she was moments short of an orgasm. Her breathing was irregular and she gasped the air into her lungs and forced it out again as quickly as she could. She opened her eyes and saw him removing his clothes. He threw them carelessly about the floor, unlike their previous two encounters when they had been neatly folded on the chair beside the bed.

Planting his knees between her legs, he stretched himself over her and she put her hands on the back of his shoulders. The bone was surrounded by well-toned muscle and she moved it gently with her hand. His cock hung heavily from him as though it could barely support its own weight. With one hand she gripped it halfway down his shaft and tentatively sheathed the foreskin back and forth. He let out a groan. His cock was dense and just a little longer than was average, in Karen's experience. The second time they had made love, she had noticed how his cock was just too long and just too wide. Inside her, it ploughed a certain and delicious line between agony and ecstasy.

The heat of his body warmed her as she masturbated him. His shaft swelled and swam in her grip and he moved his body in time with her hand. Karen drew his foreskin back completely and rubbed the head of his cock on her stomach. Alan leaned in closer and she guided his tip down to where she wanted him. Later, she would touch him all over and have him do the same to her. She would mould both their bodies into unusual positions and stimulate him until he shouted. Now, her aim was simple. She wanted him to enter her and fill her with himself.

For a minute or so, she held his shaft and worked his phallus against her pussy lips, up and down them and then in a circular pattern. She waited for the moment, the one she cherished the most. The moment when they would really connect. From two undulating areas of flesh, they would suddenly make one. Their movements would find a harmony and they would be joined. She could never tell exactly when it happened, but the noise she made was usually the best guide.

'Oh!' she cried, elongating the sound and raising the pitch as he entered her.

On into her it went, the long and wide penis. Even as it opened and stretched her, she knew it would also penetrate deeply into her. A two-way stretch. Her juices were both a lubricant and an adhesive. She felt them smooth his path into her vagina but she also felt that it was these which bound them together.

'My God!' she cried when he was fully inside her.

Karen tightened her legs around him and he began to move up and down, back and forth, slowly rocking his cock in and out of her. The beat and pulse of his movements were almost calming, as though they would send her into an ecstatic sleep, carrying her off on the wave of an orgasm. She gripped his body with her hands, his skin mature and worn by time. She thought of his years of marriage and the number of times he must have made love to his wife in that time and the way he was changing this experience into something different for her benefit. How different he was now compared with his demeanour in the shop – the gentle romance in the restaurant and now this.

His shoulders were close to hers, his arms either side of her where he supported himself on his elbows. She felt very close to him, both physically and mentally. Like a mirror image, similar areas of their bodies touched and, like a puzzle, the bits that were not similar fitted together perfectly.

She ran her hands through his hair and kissed him. He increased his motion and the gentle movements gave way to thrusts. In and out of her he went and she gripped him, feeling the walls of her vagina where he touched them with the outside of his cock, which was stony hard, the shape of it prominent in her softness. She pulled him tightly into her and squeezed with her legs as he continued to pump at her. She felt in a daze as he fucked her with a precision and a passion.

His hands moved and he scooped them under her shoulder blades, lifting her a fraction from the bed. As he pulled her tightly, she felt her flesh move with his, a sheen of sweat covering them. There was a light draft under her back where it was now separated from the bed and Karen put her elbows out behind and supported herself. The mattress moved under their exertions and it was the only noise in the room. Locked deep in the cavernous house, it might as well have been the only noise in the world.

The position of Karen's back was now at a slight angle in relation to the bed and it made Alan's cock enter her in a different way. Even though he was on top of her, smothering her almost, it gave her the sense of riding him or clinging to the front of him as though trying to scale him in some fashion. He had reared back, supporting himself on his hands, and she could see down to where they were joined. The lunges he made at her made a sound, barely discernible, but there nonetheless. It was the collection of subtleties that made sex so good for Karen. Over and above the obvious things that were there, the cut and thrust of simple fucking. Beneath it lay a whole realm of tiny movements and sounds that were the real grist of it. These all added up to something much larger than simply fucking with someone.

'Is this all right?' he asked her.

'Very,' she said, mimicking his earlier conduct in the restaurant. She wondered if he and Margaret ever talked dirty?

'Fuck me harder, Alan,' she whispered into his ear.

With a groan he began to increase his efforts. She let herself fall back on to the bed and splayed her arms out at the side of her, letting him make the pace. She felt her orgasm close by and concentrated on holding and nurturing it, making it ready to flower.

Deeply, she breathed the hot vapour they had generated and felt it turn to liquid as it touched their bodies. They were moving hard and fast, both pushing towards the same goal. She could hear how close he was to coming, the desperation and pleading in the sounds he made. She felt herself coming.

In her mind's eye, she saw it. It was a distant spot on the horizon at first, barely visible against the heated landscape of her passion. It moved into view, slowly and assuredly. The image took hold of her and she was inserted into the picture as surely as if she were there. An image that had been with her for as long as she could remember, for as long as she had been sexual. A powerful and muscled white horse galloped over the rocky landscape, brilliantly defined against the harsh background. With long and steady strides it approached her. As it neared, so she trembled and quivered, watching it and waiting for the moment when it would be with her.

It arrived and she was swept up by it. She rode it and felt it drive between her legs, the muscles pulsing and swelling with its movements. She felt the gathering speed and the rush of it against her body, the feeling of complete and absolute freedom and disconnection from everything. A single focus on a point of pure and utter pleasure. The landscape, the fire of it, the speed, everything was assimilated.

'Alan!' she cried out, holding him tightly and opening her eyes to look at him. She shook with the last vestiges of her orgasm and felt him releasing inside her.

He yelled her name into the empty silence of the room and his cock throbbed in her, the semen heavy and viscous inside her.

When they were both done, they lay and he whispered in her ear, his breath warm against it.

It was over an hour later when she jolted awake. He was there beside her, sleeping soundly and looking comfortable in his own house. His sleep had the serenity of recent sex. She lay thinking about him, about Richard and about Hamiltons.

Karen rose from the bed. She went to her attaché case. From it she took a pad and a pen and made her way quietly downstairs. She went into the large kitchen which was on the basement level and switched on the lights. She enjoyed being naked in a strange house at the dead of night. A bowl of fruit was the centre-piece of the table and Karen reached for a green apple. She went to the sink and washed it under the cold tap. She turned and was about to take a bite when she caught a glimpse of herself in the large patio door, her image shimmering like a ghost. As the reflection came back at her, naked and about to take a bite of the apple, she muttered under her breath, 'All I need now is a fig leaf.'

She went back to the table, her mind racing.

With the blank sheet of paper in front of her, the ideas began to flow. She jotted things down, doodled and made little charts here and there.

After half an hour or so, she had come up with an idea.

Chapter Five

'*OH MY GOD*, he's even more adorable on paper,' Karen said into the receiver, which was held on to her ear by the pressure of her shoulder, enabling her to leaf through the contact sheets of Maxwell and talk to Linda at the same time.

'I thought you'd be impressed,' came Linda's voice back down the line. 'That's why I printed a few shots as well, just to give you an idea.'

Any small doubt that had been in Karen's mind regarding the choices of photographer, model and location were now allayed. The three had combined wonderfully. Maxwell and the roof looked suitably intense, the bird imagery graceful and soft. Karen knew it had been a good choice and was pleased with the results.

'How come they're back so quickly?' Karen asked Linda.

'I was anxious to see what they looked like. Excited even. Maybe.' Linda was halting with her words.

'Has Maxwell seen them?'

'He loves them too,' Linda replied breezily.

Karen was unused to such a light tone from Linda, normally more prone to seriousness, and was about to remark at it when she flicked through to a picture of Maxwell emerging from the sea of doves, arms raised, and she thought better of it. She could see why Linda was so captivated.

'I can't wait to show them to Daniel,' Karen said, looking up from the photographs and out of the window of her fifth-floor office, at Sloane Square going about its business.

'Has he said anything more about the nudity?'

'No,' Karen answered. 'But if we have to, we can avoid full frontal, right?' she continued, with heavy accent on the word can.

'There's one where a dove is covering his modesty,' Linda responded unenthusiastically, 'but I think it spoils it if you go with that approach.'

'I'm hoping we won't have to, but you were wise to cover us, Linda.'

During the shoot with the falcon, Linda had taken the planned shot and some side-on shots. As Karen held them in her hands, she realised the fact his cock was not on view was almost as exciting as the full-frontal shots themselves.

'Are you going to show him all the shots, including the cover-ups?' Linda asked.

'Linda, I think the phrase cover-up is somewhat emotive.'

She heard Linda laugh down the other end of the line before she said, 'You know what I mean.'

'I know perfectly. I'm going to keep the cover-ups in reserve in case I need them. I think Daniel will be swayed. He seemed charmed by Maxwell,' Karen said.

'Everyone is. Everyone is.'

'Linda, when I've shown Daniel the prints, I'll give you a call and you should come in for lunch, okay?'

They said their goodbyes.

Karen sat and squinted at the contact sheets, wishing she had one of those small magnifying glasses she had seen professional photographers using, before turning back to the full-size prints Linda had made for her. It was Linda's not terribly subtle way of suggesting which shots they should go with. Karen trusted Linda's eye and expected her to want some feeling of control, particularly as she was used to being in complete control when it came to artistic showings of her work.

What would be the best way to approach Daniel, she wondered? Since the night at Alan's when she had so frantically begun scribbling ideas on paper, she had been thinking of the best way to communicate them to Daniel Avendon. Now she had the opportunity of showing him the photographs and if they set him in a good frame of mind, she would push ahead with her idea. If he did not like the pictures, she'd delay pitching the idea until another day. She buzzed for David. Hamiltons' offices all had old-fashioned buzzers for summoning secretaries and assistants and Karen thought they worked well, although David was not necessarily in agreement.

David entered, clipboard in hand.

'Were they the pictures?' he asked her, sitting down on the chair in front of her desk.

'Yes,' she said, handing them to him. 'I want you to look at them and then I'll ask you something.'

She studied his face as it in turn studied the images before it. She watched his eyes focus, the occasional twitch of his mouth that would give way to a smile. David was handsome in his own way and she held a great affection for him, realising at that moment that the only way she could have someone like David as her assistant was if he was gay. David closed his eyes in mock beatification before looking at Karen.

'I'm speechless,' he said.

'Now. Imagine you are Daniel Avendon. Do you like them?'

'Yes,' he said, without hesitating.

'What makes you like them?'

'They're artistic and sexy both at once. He's androgynous enough to sell the idea of the scent. It's got everything.'

'That's what I thought,' Karen said.

'Do you? Or do you think he won't like them?' David asked.

'I've got a meeting with him at twelve-thirty and I want to show him these but I also want to discuss something else with him,' Karen confided.

'So show him the pictures and if he has a wobbly, don't say anything else. You know how to handle Avendon better than me. Why ask my opinion all of a sudden?'

'I mostly wanted your take on the photos. They are gorgeous, aren't they?'

'I might have to take this one and have it done in easy-wipe formica laminate,' David said, swooping up a picture of Maxwell with the falcon gripping the gauntlet, the bird seeming to stare at the leather hood Maxwell wore.

'Sometimes, David . . .' she said in a warning tone.

He placed the picture back on her desk and looked at his clipboard, switching into business mode.

'Avendon at twelve-thirty, like you say,' he said to her. 'This afternoon we should go down to The Dungeon and finalise what's going to happen with the underwear promotion. They want the boxers out of the stock-room next weekend, not the weekend after, and want us to roll forward.'

'Fine. We've done no advertising for it, but what the hell?'

'Alan Saxton called for you while you were on the phone. No message. A woman called and wouldn't leave her name or a message. I tried to wheedle one out of her, but she said she'd call back.'

'Young, old?' Karen asked him.

'Sounded young, a bit mousy. I'm not good on ages even if they're standing in front of me. On the phone . . .' he raised his shoulders indicating the difficulty this would add.

'That everything?'

'Almost,' he answered. 'I booked you Virgin Upper Class to New York on the flight you wanted. The return's for the Thursday but I can extend it if you want. Four days doesn't seem like long.'

'It is, believe me,' she told him.

Three or four times a year, Karen went to New York to look at potential campaigns she could run. Most of Hamiltons' more successful of these normally involved the States. Several European-themed promotions and two from Africa had worked well, but none as well as America. America sells, was one of Daniel's favourite sayings. Avendon loved America, New York in particular, and Karen quickly caught on that it was a good way to stay on his best side. While there, she would visit three or four of her usual contacts, gathering ideas and leaving the ultimate legwork to the buyers at Hamiltons. She hoped to be able to put the trip to good use, especially if her meeting with Avendon went well at twelve-thirty.

'I'll be around the shop for the next hour or so if you need me,' she told him. 'My pager will be on, just like a doctor on call . . .'

Karen went around to the other side of the fifth floor and into Alan Saxton's office, the door of which was ajar. Alan sat there, leaning back in his chair with his chin supported by his strong hand. He was deep in thought and Karen knew that he hadn't noticed her enter. His office seemed more old-fashioned and musty than her own, dating him slightly although he was still far from stuffy. His desk was a picture of order and efficiency, a blotter and a pen set with a marble base, the usual paper clips and bulldog clips dotted around. There was no picture of his ex-wife in evidence and Karen wondered if there had been one on the other times she had been in his office. She racked her brain but could not remember.

It was only when Karen closed the door that his concentration broke. He looked at her and she saw his expression lift, going from one of serious thought to pleasure at the sight of her.

'You look light years away, not just a million miles,' she said to him, her voice light. 'Are you okay?'

'I'm fine, really,' he said, getting to his feet and

coming round the desk to plant a short kiss on her cheek. He seemed to have a problem with the sort of middle-distance intimacy where they were not in public but not having sex.

'David said you called.'

'Oh yes, I did,' he replied, as though that had jogged his memory. 'I've got something for you.'

He reached into the drawer of his desk and produced a book. He handed it to her. Karen looked at it. It was by one of her favourite authors.

'I didn't know this was out yet,' she said to him.

'It isn't,' he responded, looking pleased with himself. 'I have a friend who works at her publisher's in the States. She sent it over for me. It won't be out over there for another month. I know you like her and I thought you could read it on the plane.'

She grinned at him and looked at the book. 'It comes all the way over here only for me to take it back again. How indulgent.'

'I'm supposed to say you're worth it, or some such phrase at this point, I assume?'

'It's not mandatory, Alan.'

'Will I see you before you go?'

'It might be difficult. We're going to do the boxer shorts promo a week earlier, which is a bit of a pain. I'll let you know.'

He looked at her and she felt a twinge of guilt go through her. She told herself to stop it. Alan was an adult and so was she. They knew what they were doing. However, he did not know what she was doing with Richard. She was about to ask him why he had been so rapt when she first walked in but was interrupted by her pager.

'I have to go. Thanks for the book,' she said, clutching it to her. He smiled at her.

Dispatching David quickly, she filled the time in between her meeting with Avendon by wandering through the store and talking to the staff, doing what she called her woman-of-the-people bit. It was more

51

than just a PR stunt for Karen. She loved Hamiltons and enjoyed simply walking through it, soaking it up. Just before she was due to see Daniel, she returned to her office and looked through the photographs of Maxwell once more. She now felt confident they would please Avendon and put him in a good frame of mind.

Daniel Avendon's corner office on the fifth floor was breathtaking. It could be seen from Sloane Square, protruding slightly from one side behind the turret like a small glass extension to the building. With two walls made from nothing but glass, it let the light flood in. The furniture was lush, an eclectic mixture that he had collected on his travels, bringing it all together in his office and making each piece fit with the other. Just like he did with everything, the overseer of all the pieces on the board.

'What's the essence of Hamiltons?' he asked her as soon as she had entered, not even giving her the chance to say hello or sit down. She made her way to her usual chair.

'Ambiguity. Fun. Eccentricity. Class. Choice.'

'And the fragrance will convey all this?'

'And vice versa, Daniel. It conveys us and we convey it.'

He seemed satisfied. She watched the way he would suddenly develop a nagging feeling about something that he would make someone else allay for him. Then he would change tack completely, the thought apparently buried.

'Do we have much of an agenda today?' he asked her.

We certainly do, she thought.

'Linda Cole sent the contact sheets and a few prints she had made.'

She handed them to him, not committing herself to an opinion in advance of his.

'Fine. Excellent,' he said as he took the envelope.

Karen tried to read his face, to get a sense from his

expression of what was going on in his mind as he surveyed the images before him. His eyebrows were intense and his whole brow furrowed while his eyes dragged over the picture. Whatever he decided would hold sway. That was the way of things. She was thankful that he had an interest in photography and would no doubt be evaluating the shots seriously, with the eye of a collector.

'Linda Cole. Wonderful. She has such an excellent eye and the composition of the shots is delightful. The boy will sell this. Which order do you plan to use the three shots in?'

'Originally, I thought it would be good to use the one with the doves first. But now I think it would be nice to start with the hooded picture, where you can't see it's him, and then use the over-the-shoulder angel shot and finish with the doves. Slowly revealing him. What do you think?' she asked him.

'The doves would be a nice climax. Good. It sounds fine.' He appeared happy.

'And you like the shots?' she asked, not sure if she should push him too much.

'Yes. Have you scheduled New York?'

'I go out on Sunday. I've been in touch with Madeleine and also with George. They're both available to meet. I think a New England style clothes thing would go over well in the Autumn. We've never really done that whole L L Bean, J Crew thing.'

'It's not too Ralph Lauren?' he asked her.

'I don't think we'd do it in quite that way, Daniel,' she told him.

'True. We'd have to do more than just clothes, though.'

'Sure. There'd be a whole lifestyle concept to it, the usual sort of thing. We could run advertorials, food promotions. There's mileage in it.'

'And you would like to do this in the Autumn, or should I say Fall?'

'That's the most obvious time to do it, although I've

53

been thinking about something else as well, perhaps a little more permanent.'

'Permanent?' he asked, raising an eyebrow.

She went into it.

'It's a high concept kind of idea. It's aimed at women and I think it's something they'd all appreciate.'

'Which is?'

'Eden without the Adam.'

She continued while the previous sentence was still nesting itself in his mind.

'Shopping for women only. A department catering specifically to their, our, needs and wants. A fun place to shop where you'd come with a group of friends. We could call it The Garden, as in Eden.'

'Interesting.'

'Specially selected products and staff. A well thought-out shopping experience from beginning to end. Not just where they offer you a coffee or mineral water. Something more committed and, well, honest.'

Avendon was about to say something when his intercom buzzer went. Karen was annoyed that her flow had been broken. Avendon would not normally let himself be disturbed. He leaned over and pushed the button.

'Yes?'

'Gabrielle is here, Mr Avendon.'

'Tell her I'll be with her as soon as I can.'

'She's insisting that she sees you now, Mr Avendon.'

'I will only be another ten or fifteen minutes, Jane. Tell her to wait.' Avendon was becoming irked.

'But, sir . . .'

The intercom went abruptly dead, as though Jane had been strangled or stabbed. The door to Avendon's office swung open. Karen decided not to turn her head when the door opened. She remained seated and tried to relax and fight the angry feeling that was taking her over. It was the first time in all of her meetings with Daniel that his secretary had even dared to buzz him. She gripped the side of the chair, her knuckles

54

whitening, before her survival instincts kicked in more consciously and her face assumed a relaxed mask that wore a gentle smile.

Into her field of vision came a woman in her mid- to late-fifties who would once, Karen thought, have been glamorous. Now she looked as though her life story was sculpted into her features and engraved on to her skin, an outward sign of some inner turmoil, quite what Karen could not wonder, being more concerned with exactly *who* she was. She wore a sweeping blue dress that would have been more at home at a party or even on a panto dame and Karen pondered whether this was a studied eccentricity along the lines of Vivienne Westwood or simply bad taste, her gut reaction veering towards the latter assumption.

'Karen, this is my sister, Gabrielle.' Avendon was on his feet and Karen followed, looking at the sister and trying to see the resemblance.

'He means half-sister,' the woman said, not extending a hand, 'but that always leads to some nasty remark from him. I'm glad to see he's learned.'

'Pleased to meet you, Gabrielle. I'm Karen Taylor.' She put her hand out and continued. 'I run the promotions . . .'

Karen got no further. The woman had turned from her and went to look out of the window.

'The view doesn't change much,' she said, speaking to the glass rather than to anyone in the room. 'Very little does, here.'

'Gabrielle worked in the shop for a time, in the late Sixties,' Avendon said to Karen with an apologetic look on his face.

'Worked in the shop?' she said, turning, emphasising the questioning nature of her statement. 'You make it sound like I did make-overs. I owned, still do, fifteen per cent of the stock. The unsilent partner, you used to refer to me as.'

'It was noisy partner. Actually,' Avendon responded, scratching his forehead and squinting, as though used to such verbal jousting with his half-sister.

'Should I come back later, Daniel?' Karen asked him.

'Please, don't let me interrupt. I'll return to my window view and you can carry on,' Gabrielle said to Daniel as though Karen had not even spoken.

'Daniel, I'd rather talk about it when you have more time.'

Karen looked at the woman and thought about giving her a quick shove through the glass.

'Please. Do finish, Karen. It sounded exciting and I'm sure Gabrielle would not mind waiting outside.'

Gabrielle had gone back to her window view as she said she would and did not appear about to go anywhere. Karen licked her lips, which felt dry, and tried to think on her feet, willing for David to page her at that precise second.

'Daniel. I have to go. I'll talk to you later.' She was firm and precise in her tone and nodded at him as though the physical movement of her head would lodge the meaning of her words into him. As she did so, Gabrielle turned and gave a smile which was small, barely discernible but triumphant nonetheless.

Karen left quickly and closed the door, heading straight for Alan Saxton's office.

'Alan, who the fuck is Gabrielle?' she practically shouted at him.

'You've met her then?'

'Met her? She crashed a meeting with Daniel, right in the middle of something. His half-sister?' She raised her arms as she spoke.

'I'll close the door,' he said, standing and crossing the room.

He returned and sat in his chair with a resigned sigh. Karen saw him gather his thoughts and take a breath.

'Daniel has told you the old Dick Foxton story? I've been there when he has, I think?' he asked.

'Yes, I've heard it only once and as an anecdote. All that old-fashioned bitter rivalry between his father and another store owner. It sounds like an Ealing comedy.'

'Gabrielle and Daniel have the same mother, Mary. Mary was married to Daniel's father Lawrence and to Dick Foxton, Gabrielle's father.'

'What happened to Dick Foxton?' she questioned.

'He was killed in a motor racing accident. Fast cars were a passion for him. Mary was married to him at the time and Gabrielle was only four years old. Only eight months after Dick Foxton died, she married Lawrence Avendon and a year later, Daniel was born. I think a lot of people thought that Mary must have been having an affair with Lawrence Avendon long before Dick Foxton died.'

'How does all of that result in Gabrielle having a fifteen per cent stake in Hamiltons?'

'Daniel never says very much, but I think Lawrence and Mary had an absolutely horrible time of a marriage. They separated when he was only five. Lawrence kept custody of Daniel and I suspect the buy-off was a stake in Hamiltons for Gabrielle. At the time Dick Foxton died, his store was in bad shape and closed not long after his death, so there was no real money for Mary or Gabrielle to fall back on.'

'And did Mary get any benefit from this?'

'She was looked after. Daniel made some alteration to her trust fund in the late Sixties and I administered it up until she died in nineteen-eighty.' Alan's tone was even.

'God. I thought we were just a small, well-respected department store with a reputation for eccentricity. We're in the wrong business. We should be making a soap opera. What does her fifteen per cent add up to?'

'In sheer commercial terms, not a lot. The deal was structured to enable her type of share capital to give her a good income and little real involvement. Lawrence Avendon was a bastard and made sure that Dick Foxton's offspring wouldn't get any piece of his beloved Hamiltons. In practice, however, I think she can make life awkward, especially as she has hooks into Daniel.'

'This is going to fuck things up, I can tell.'

'What do you mean?' he asked her.

She shook her head, exhaling through her nose. 'Nothing. Thanks for filling me in on all of this. And thank you again for that book.'

Karen sat in her office for half an hour, staring at nothing, thinking of nothing in particular, having instructed David not to disturb her under any circumstances. 'Not even for Daniel?' he had asked her. 'Especially not if it's Daniel,' had been her reply.

Picking up the receiver she called Daniel and was put through to him instantly.

'I've been trying to reach you,' he said 'but I was told you were not to be interrupted. Are you that mad at me?'

'Did you like the idea?' she asked, ignoring his attempt to be winsome.

'I think it will sell. This is a big project. You should produce a proposal of some sort. When you have a rough draft, talk to Alan about costings and we'll schedule a meeting after you are back from New York. I think that, providing the cost analysis works, you'll have your Eden without Adam.'

'Thank you,' she said, wondering if it was really going to be that simple.

She finished her day by taking a last look at Maxwell and then going out on to the roof, watching the light change over London. She stooped and from the gravel retrieved a single white dove feather. She put it in her pocket and left.

Chapter Six

AS KAREN STEPPED into the taxi, Richard had his head in the front window, giving the driver an address in North London. She settled back on to the black leather of the seat, which had been worn shiny and looked not far from splitting. She saw the driver's eyes in the mirror, flicking up and then trying to peer down and get a view of her legs. She pulled the dress down, not because of the driver, but to cover what she had on underneath, not wanting Richard to see. The dress was a short slip in a lamé that was almost pewter in colour, hanging from her shoulders by the thinnest of straps. The nipples of her bare breasts pointed out with a sexy prominence and the shortness of the skirt showed off the muscular shapeliness of her legs to its fullest.

Richard joined her, placing his jacket carefully on the seat next to him. Not wanting to risk Alan seeing them and needing to change in any case, Karen had made him pick her up from her flat. She had pushed her short hair back as much as she could with the help of some mousse and she had kept the lines of her make-up thin, giving her the same metallic look as the dress. She wore no jewellery and the impression, almost correct, was that with one small cut to each of the straps, she would be completely naked except for the silver stilettos. There was still her underwear, of course, but it was a long ride to North London.

'You look like a little rocket girl,' Richard said to her.

'How do you mean?'

'Like something from the Jetsons or even the Flintstones. Sort of wild. Don't walk near any magnets.'

He beamed at her, pushing at his hair, and she felt a quiver run through her, forgetting that she was in a taxi.

'You look quite harsh yourself,' she said, rubbing the leg of his grey trousers.

'This is meant to be a soft line. Like a blunt blade.'

'I see. Is it one of ours?'

'We just started stocking them. Krizia.'

'Is this the long narrow line in suits I keep reading about?' she asked him sarcastically.

'Everyone wants a long suit at the moment. All we did was pull the trousers up on the mannequins to make the jackets look longer, and it works. This is a proper long suit, of course.'

'Of course.'

'Nice, huh?'

'Yes,' she said, almost biting at the word. It would be her last chance to see him before she flew to New York at the weekend and already the four days she would be there felt a long time to be away. From Hamiltons, from The Garden, from Richard and from Alan. For the moment, she concentrated only on Richard in the taxi beside her.

A grey waistcoat matched the trousers and the jacket so neatly folded on the seat; a three-piece suit underpinned by a white T-shirt. It was loose around him, revealing different angles and aspects of him as he moved. Very London in late Summer. They were both deliberately dressed up, ready for a night of dancing and posing at the opening of a new jazz club in Islington. Karen wanted to blow off steam and had already been to the gym early that morning, releasing a lot of pressure, but some partying and some sex with Richard would finish things off nicely. When she came back from New York, she would be ready to give Daniel a full, uninterrupted pitch for The Garden, without any gatecrashers.

Karen turned her mind to Richard, wanting to enjoy him while she had him. She knew he would ask the question eventually. She waited and a minute passed, but he did not disappoint her.

'Are you wearing knickers under there?' he asked lasciviously, gripping her thigh and squeezing it. She slapped his hand away playfully.

'I've got you a present,' she said to him.

'Where? Not in that little Chanel bag?' he asked, motioning towards it at the same time.

'No.'

'Where then?'

She hitched one side of her skirt up and revealed the leg of a soft pure cotton boxer short and then pushed it back down again.

'John Smedley underwear from Harrods. Contraband,' she said huskily.

Karen glanced up and met the eyes of the taxi driver in his rear-view mirror; his gaze quickly averted as their eyes met in glass. Richard, meanwhile, gawped at her and then laughed.

'You are so naughty,' he said to her.

'It's the most gorgeous soft natural cotton. You wouldn't know you were wearing them,' she purred at him. 'Maybe I won't be, soon. Feel how soft.' She raised the side of her skirt again, positioning her leg so it was easier for him to touch, but not making her movements too obvious to the driver, who she knew was watching everything.

Against the side of her leg, his fingers brushed the skin and then came to the border of the boxer shorts. Richard popped his index finger under the hem and into the ridge of muscle on her outer thigh, letting his digit travel up until it was at the top of her leg. She turned her head and looked at him as the taxi made its way through the traffic, the sounds of the evening simmered by the heat of the waning sun. They looked at each other, both resisting the urge to kiss, and he removed his finger, letting his whole hand move around to drop between her legs, resting on the seat in front of her crotch. The outside of his hand was against her inner thighs, close to her pussy, which was beginning to moisten. His finger lighted on the material where it covered her sex and then the hand was gone.

She leaned over and whispered to him, 'There's a slit right down the front of these.' She let her words sink in. 'And I've left the fly button undone.'

In the mirror, the driver's eyes were darting wildly about in their sockets as if he were trying to follow a fly. Karen moved her rear forward on the seat by several inches and leaned back, positioning her legs just provocatively enough. Richard picked up his jacket, pretended to look through it for something and then when he had finished, placed it on her lap. The wool was surprisingly gentle against her legs. The motion of the vehicle shifted her from side to side, a rocking action that was soothing and sexual at once; the feeling of her nudity under the metal-coloured dress, only the boxer shorts holding her in check. Inside them, her pussy was damp and ready for him.

Casually, Richard's right hand made its way across the seat, as though it had a life all its own, a force he could not control. As the hand moved, he simply looked ahead or out of the side window, seemingly unaware of what his hand was up to. Its journey was agonisingly slow, like a snake stalking its prey, the movement agile and unhurried and his little finger twitching from time to time. She stared at it as though it were disembodied from him, nothing to do with him as it made its way closer. It disappeared under the portion of the jacket that hung off the side of her left leg on to the seat. She waited for his touch but it did not come. The taxi seemed silent and she turned and frowned at him. He smiled at her, teasingly.

She jolted when he touched the side of her leg, an involuntary spasm seizing her. One finger quickly turned into two and then three and before long his whole hand was resting on her leg, feeling a degree cooler than her own flesh, which had taken on a feverish heat. A few circular motions on her leg above the knee and then his hand was off, journeying under the jacket on her lap, up the front of the top half of her leg and under the rim of the skirt. It made contact with the velvety cotton of the underwear and he brought it to rest on the curve of her inner thigh, close to her crotch. And then nothing but the same smile.

Karen sat in the taxi with the jacket on her lap and Richard's hand up her skirt. That was the exterior. On the inside, she felt herself boiling with desire, the shorts getting damper by the second. Like they were playing a game of poker, they both sat still, moved only by the motion of the taxi. Karen was confident she would hold out longer than he could. Richard was a novice tease. She set her face into a relaxed expression, as if enjoying a pleasant ride in the countryside, gazing out of the window.

The hand spread out over her pussy like a shadow casting itself across her. It cupped her, fitting easily with the shape of her body, cradling her. He had found one of the small white buttons that should have held the fly of the shorts in check and he was twirling it between his fingers. Karen felt her pubic hair sprouting from the slit in the front and the static tickle of Richard's fingers as they grazed it. The heat between her legs was intense and her rear felt glued to the seat of the cab. His attention turned from the button to *her* as his fingers scratched at her hair, the soft puffy mons beneath it, which he pushed his fingers into. As he delicately caressed his fingers against her pubic hair, the fly on the shorts opened wider and her sex was bared beneath the dress.

Richard's movements were discreet and careful, as if he were performing microsurgery or defusing a bomb. The jacket on her lap barely moved, bobbing up and then down again only occasionally, as he worked delicately at her with the fingers of his right hand.

Karen alternated glances between Richard, the jacket and the rear-view mirror of the driver, his eyes seemingly never far from it. The track made by his fingers increased, spreading out over her crotch, both up, down and across it, running themselves over the available surface area, gliding over her but never entering, merely tormenting her.

In a first outward display, Karen inhaled deeply through her nose, the oxygen filling her head and clearing it, her senses becoming more attuned to Richard and to his hand. He seemed to take the breath as a sign and he cautiously poked a finger between the wet lips of her pussy, which accommodated him with ease and eagerness. She was well lubricated and pliant to his precise touch. Her clitoris swelled and Richard caressed it briefly, trailing his hand along the slit made by her lips. When his fingers were at the bottom of the fly hole, she felt him reach and grip the material of the boxer shorts and then pull them upwards from between her legs, the fabric tightening around her rear and gathering up in a tight stretch on her sex.

She smothered her cry by placing her hand to her face and holding her breath in, her legs quivering as Richard continued to pull the underwear up into the crack of her pussy, gathering a steady rhythm that echoed its way through her. As he coyly tugged the cloth up and down between her legs, she let the passion swell in her, all the time maintaining a cool exterior, not forgetting that she was in the back of a taxi riding through London in the evening rush-hour. The cloth was soft and damp against her, the nap of it maddeningly stimulating.

Richard released his grip on the boxers and placed his finger through the slit and into her pussy, his palm close to her clitoris. Karen let her legs droop apart as his finger slipped into her, a slick and experienced probe that explored her depths. He positioned his hand so that it formed a cage over her crotch that could remain still while only the middle finger, inside her,

64

did its work, like a tiny piston reaming her pussy. She wondered if the position of his hand, cramped over her, was painful for him, although the speed and fluidity of his finger gave no indication that it was.

No words had passed between them and Karen stared at the jacket on her lap as though mesmerised by it, waiting for it to move. But it did not. She could feel him fingering her but that was all. Neither of them gave any apparent sign of what they were doing. She continued to watch the jacket, Richard's arm across the seat and his hand buried under it, clawed over her pussy with his middle finger pushing in and out of her. Other cars passed them or the cab overtook someone; people on the pavements wandering or rushing about; everyone oblivious to them and what they were doing; except for the driver. He knew what they were up to and had been observing them in his mirror since she had first got into the taxi. Karen could see enjoyment in the intensity of his eyes.

Her breathing became short, intense but quiet pants escaping her. Richard had increased the speed at which his finger was moving in her and had changed the direction of the pressure, pushing more upwards to the underside of her clitoris. She reached across and briefly stroked the back of his neck, the hair slightly bristly like a brush. Returning both hands to her sides, she concentrated on herself and the feelings that were stoking up in her, needing release.

The back of a taxi was, she supposed, an unusual place to feel such passion, but in that single moment it seemed perfect. She was in contrast to her surroundings – the inside of the car, the traffic and the frantic rush of London itself. With the movements of his finger, Richard had at first created a frenetic pace in her but now she was ready to let that break into a long and delightful release, like a high diver free-falling through the air before finally hitting the water.

A twitch in her legs was the first sign. Her rear tightened and it lifted her up in the seat. Richard's finger was now massaging her vagina and clitoris deeply, roving between them and spreading her, making her squirm away from it and towards it by turns. Her hands gripped the edge of the black leather seat and her body tensed itself as though contracting towards some invisible centre.

She gritted her teeth as she came, her vagina rippling and her eyelids falling heavily shut. She fought the urge to clench her whole face and wail, instead forcing her eyes open and glimpsing the driver's eyes in the mirror, on hers the whole time. She kept her eyes open and locked them on the driver's as her body made very tiny convulsions, a brake on her orgasm that filtered it out slowly. It felt as though the orgasm had gushed into her from nowhere and she was now filled to the brim with it, forcing it out with high pressure through the very small actions she had permitted herself.

Richard's finger slowed and finally stopped, slipping itself out of her and from under the dress and jacket. Karen saw sweat on the back of the driver's neck and also on Richard's brow.

Carefully and quickly, she raised her bottom and pulled off the boxer shorts, damp and sweaty from her juices, knowing exactly what they would leave the driver as a tip.

Chapter Seven

HAVING FREE RUN of a large and well-furnished apartment in Greenwich Village was a luxury Karen planned to make full use of. Not that she had managed to yet. She had been in New York for a day and a half, her time split between the obvious places in the garment district around West 34th Street and several irregular hours spent in bed beating the jet lag. The next day, she planned to spend some time venturing to Queens or the other way to New Jersey. She would not have considered herself a well-seasoned Manhattanite, but she had been enough times to feel comfortable and to enjoy herself. Now she wanted to take in her immediate surroundings.

The apartment belonged to Jake, a friend who was a video director with his own successful production company. Jake was attempting to make the jump from music videos and advertisements into movies, the reason his apartment was empty while he was in Los Angeles. She had stayed with him once before, but in a different apartment on Central Park West. Jake obviously felt the Village was the place to be, in addition to Los Angeles. Jake left the key with the doorman who had played deliberately hard to convince when she arrived, but soon succumbed. Karen knew she was expected but he had enjoyed stringing her along and she enjoyed playing the game.

Karen sat in the main room of the apartment, nibbling on blue corn tortilla chips. With Jake not there, she felt like a burglar with an invitation, certain the police would rush in on her at any moment and accuse her of something. Even the silence in a strange house sounded different. Fresh from a post-shopping-trip shower, she wore a thick blue towelling robe that had been laid out on the guest bed when she arrived. From her grocery bag, yet to be unpacked, she pulled a diet cherry soda.

The time away from Hamiltons was helping to get her thoughts in order. Away from the bustle of the shop she was able to think clearly about what she wanted The Garden to be like, how it would look and feel. It gave her the chance to visualise it unhampered. At other moments, she had thought about Richard and about Alan. The distance between her and them was not as helpful in giving her a clear picture. Whenever she thought of one, the other popped up too, as though they were inseparable in her mind and she was unable to have one without the other. Unless she had neither. Karen put her thoughts on hold.

She found her way up the main stairwell, on the opposite side to the one that led to the guest's wing. The apartment was particularly well designed for guests, with a suitable number of bathrooms and spare bedrooms. Jake enjoyed hosting people, she knew, even *in absentia*. The robe that had been laid out when she arrived had a long note left on top explaining where everything was and that she should help herself to anything she needed.

She wandered past the main bedroom, to a door at the end of the landing. It was unlike the other doors in the house, Karen could tell, as it seemed set into the frame in the way a sauna door would be. On the floor outside it, tucked close to the door and almost obscured by shadow, was a remote control with a Post-It note stuck on it. Karen picked it up and read it.

K, once inside the room, use the remote and go through the numbers sequentially. It's the only way – and a teaser. Have fun, J.

Karen looked at the remote control unit in her hand. The buttons on it were numbered from one to five plus a red button on the top right. The controller had nothing else on it but the five numbered black buttons and the one red. She smiled, flicked the light switch on the wall outside and opened the door of the room. It was heavy and swung inwards with a precision and weight that suggested well-oiled hinges or hydraulics. Harsh fluorescent light flickered, giving a strobe effect to the room, making it impossible to tell what was in there. Karen stood in the doorway until the light finally clicked into full brightness.

The whole room was banked with televisions, from floor to ceiling. As Karen turned to close the door, she was amazed to see that it had three television monitors down it, accounting for the weight. She pushed it to and was surrounded by screens, all with red standby lights beaconing silently from them. The room was small, but not claustrophobic – about twelve feet square.

'Oh boy,' she muttered. 'This is like science fiction.'

Under her bare feet the maroon carpet was made up of carpet tiles, a foot square and with a deep luxurious pile to them. The light was glaring and unforgiving, like the lights over a dentist's chair or some of the lighting they experimented with at the shop. Alone in the room, the screens lifeless and waiting, the silence broken only by the whistle of air-conditioning, she felt a stirring in her groin, not unlike one she had resisted earlier, in the shower.

Looking down at the controller, she studied its simplistic design. It was a TV remote control with five large channel change buttons. There were no controls for volume or brightness. She pushed the red standby button, wondering where to aim it. She just held it above her head, realising as she looked up that even the ceiling had monitors embedded into it.

Slowly and with no particular order, the red lights disappeared, replaced by green dots. The room lights, which ran around the point where walls met ceiling, dimmed down to a much more accommodating and friendly glow. There were a few audible clicks and then the hiss and crackle of static as the screens came to life. All the red standby lights had now extinguished but the screens merely showed black. The lights remained at the same level.

Karen pushed the button numbered one on the control pad, as that seemed to be the most logical thing to do. Gradually music started to fade in. Each of the four walls and the ceiling acted as a single screen, showing a video. Karen recognised it as a popular boy band, one of the many that had spawned from the clubs and into the bedrooms of millions of young girls via Saturday morning television. There was a digital clock on the bottom right corner spinning with the precision required for video editing. Karen wondered if Jake had actually directed this one. It was not a song she particularly cared for although the band members more than made up for that. She liked to look at their flesh, and it had been edited in a way just titillating enough to make her feel the pulse of herself against the robe. Fast cutting shots showed glimpses of torso, smiles and camaraderie. Karen wished she was Jake, able to play with these images however he chose in the editing room.

The walls rhythmically changed so that each of them split into four, quadrupling the images at once. Then they switched to each single monitor with the same image on them, making the size of the pictures in front of her eyes vary in time with the music and choreography.

The screens went abruptly blank. Karen could hear her quickened heart in the closeted atmosphere of the room. She looked down at the remote and pushed button number one again to get the images back.

Nothing happened. She thought about Jake's note and the need to press the buttons in sequence. Karen pushed button three – again, nothing. Jake was a teaser. When she touched button two, she heard the speakers come back to life, a faint sound of breathing on them.

On the screen the black gave way as the image faded up. It was the boy band again. One of them at least, one of the backing singers – a shot of the side of his face and shoulders. He was lying on his back, on a bed, grimacing and sweating, turning his head from side to side every now and then. As the camera pulled back, it revealed a woman astride him and they fucked with the familiar, practised motion of lovers, their bodies rolling in similar directions as their movements quickened and complemented each other.

Karen stood and stared with her mouth open, gawping at the tight sinewy flesh and failing to believe what was in front of her eyes. The wall was one single image of the two of them fucking away furiously and wordlessly. Then the bank of monitors split into two halves, on the horizontal, the top half preserving the view of the bed, the bottom half a close-up of a cock entering a pussy, mercilessly back and forth, the vagina expanding as it did so. The timing between the two images was perfect, a unison of thrusting.

Like a window, the wall went into four squares, the two figures thrashing on the bed and the close-up of the pussy remaining on the top two. They were joined at the bottom by a close in shot of the backing singer's head pushing itself into the pillow. On the final quarter, the video of the band's latest single played. As the song approached its climax, so did the couple on the bed. Karen saw the contortion on the face, the cock sliding out of the quivering pussy and the singer sitting up abruptly. His body rigid, the singer came into mid-air, the video freeze-framing, back-tracking and repeating the ejaculation in a sequence that seemed endless. Threads of come forming on the taut bronze flesh of his stomach, his cries just audible as the music began to fade.

And then blackness again.

This time, the silence was broken by Karen's panting. Through all of it she had been rubbing at herself with the robe, not certain her eyes were telling the truth. She felt under the robe and was wet and swollen, the lips of her pussy covered in fluid. She gathered some on a fingertip and licked it. She wished she had made the most of the video while it had been there, instead of just gawping. Knowing it was pointless, Karen tried to restore the image using the controller. It was time to move on. She undid the robe, dropped it to the floor and sat on it, legs crossed, her sex alive and heavy in between them, waiting to see what button number three held in store.

A bass drum started, insistent and thudding, one, two, three, four. The music had a dirty, masturbatory rhythm to it.

If she had gawped before, now her mouth almost fell like a lead weight. On the screen, to the music, a single solitary male figure was lying on a bed, stroking and caressing himself. Hands running over the delicate body, tweaking at his own nipples and cupping his balls in his hands. Through all of the movements, the hands eventually came back to concentrate on the large erect penis that glistened as though from the application of an oil. All of that would have been enough to send Karen off into a fantasy from which the only outcome would be orgasm.

But, there was more.

The image that had haunted her for the last two weeks, that had been there when she made love with Richard and with Alan, was there before her on the screen in a raw and explicit way that even her subconscious had been unable to process adequately in her dreams. This was her dream made electric and twelve feet high and she was both dwarfed by its size and smothered by its expanse. She drowned in the image.

It was Maxwell.

Lazily and unhurriedly, he lay on a large oval bed, his body against a background of crisp white cotton, masturbating himself. Karen watched his hand and the rhythm that seemed so accustomed to the pace of his own desire as he beat himself. His torso moved slightly, indicating the flurry of movement that she hoped would follow shortly. The drum beat on, going through her. His dainty, thin hands and body were the perfect counterpoint to the sharp picture of ecstasy he wore on his face, his nose scrunched up and his teeth showing.

It was a different sort of arousal to that she had felt previously, watching the band member fucking. This image generated a heat in her that permeated her skin from the inside to the out, making its slowest journey on her face, where her cheeks were red and flushed.

Karen slowly worked a finger into herself, feeling the outline and shape of her sex around her digit. She lay back and raised her knees higher to make herself more open and round. As the finger slid into the second knuckle, she let out a gasp and closed her eyes. Straining her arm further forward and down between her legs, she moved her finger in deep enough to feel as though she held herself in the palm of her hand. She kept her position and then opened her eyes and looked at Maxwell on the ceiling monitors, massaging himself in keeping with his hunger. All the while his cock quivered and pulsated. Karen worked at her clitoris, her pussy feeling closer and closer to her own face as her body bent to allow her finger entry. She closed her eyes again, holding Maxwell in her mind, wanting to edit him in her head.

When next she opened her eyes, ready to flood her sight with him and push herself to orgasm, the image had gone and the music was dwindling. She continued to work on herself, not knowing if she should release herself now or wait in case there were yet more images to come for her and carry her off. She wanted to come, but more than that she wanted to push buttons four and five. Karen gritted her teeth and removed her finger as she sat upright, blinking at the empty banks of screens in front of her.

Perhaps she had imagined it, her aching desire for Maxwell and her feverish imagination combining and ending up displayed on the screen, as though the image up there was a reflection of the one in her mind. That would have been pure bliss, she thought, to have been able to make her mental images appear on the screen, although she could not tell exactly what they would be.

She pushed button four, but not before giving button three a quick try to see if she could retrieve Maxwell from wherever he was stored.

This time it was much more conventional. A melange of different images danced before her eyes. On each screen a different fantasy. A man entering a woman from behind, the both of them making strained faces from the exertions of sex. Three people stood in a line, a woman in the middle of two men throwing her head back and letting her tongue protrude. A woman standing on tip-toe gripped handles high on a wall whilst a tall man gently gripped her hips and entered her with his large phallus.

Karen's finger was back inside herself and she concentrated on her clitoris. She rolled around on the floor to see different walls and what they showed. She lay on her side, then on her back. She crouched and looked in front of her. All around, a frenzy of sexual activity. She felt lifted by the static energy and the rush of all the sensory input, as if she were running a small charge through her own body. Her pussy was humming, needing to be filled. She concentrated on her clitoris, rubbing it harder and faster, the strokes getting shorter. Now she was on her knees, sweat running down the bridge of her nose, and she was about to come. She rolled over to her left side and her elbow, furious from the force of masturbation, banged the controller. She was shocked when a small door in the floor opened.

Scuttling back, she was startled by the way the carpet tile had suddenly shifted to one side, revealing a small mirror less than a foot or so square. She peered at it like a cat that had been scared, her sweaty reflection looking back at her.

On the walls, people were at each other madly. They were licking, sucking, rubbing and penetrating each other, using their own bodies and the bodies of others in a desperate frenzy. Her senses were overloaded with stimuli. Somewhere between her tight clitoris and her slowly widening vagina, she was gripped by a force that held her in a precarious balance.

Karen stood and squatted over the mirror, looking at her pussy in it, the trail of her buttocks and then her hand. Her face became a scowl as she explored herself and watched the whole process in the mirror.

Glancing down at her image and then up on to the screens, she ran her fingers over the lips of her pussy, stroking her clitoris. Karen chose to focus on one particular image on a monitor. It happened to be the screen that was easiest for her to see in her current position, but she also found the image exciting. A woman was suspended from silken scarves, wrists bound to ankles, hanging like a pendulum. A man stood, his thick cock deep inside the hanging figure, and rocked her back and forth on to his member. The woman in the sling threw her head back with pleasure as though on a swing.

Karen turned her attention to the mirror for a few moments and when she looked back up at the screen, the woman in the sling was gone. On the outside screens, forming a border around the central section, countless images were cut together, impossible to focus on but subliminally exciting. In the centre, on four screens, was a pussy that was filmed from beneath. Karen halted her own movements to watch the screen, removing her hand from herself.

The figure on the television stopped also, the hand there disappearing.

Karen put her hand under herself and her own hand came into view on the screen. Tentatively, she manipulated herself, all the time watching the identical image on the screen.

Focusing on two things, the screen with the picture of her pussy and her pussy itself, Karen touched herself harder and faster, the backs of her thighs banging on to her sweaty calf muscles, back arched and clitoris crying out between her fingers. She expelled her breaths sharply and made a desperate squeaking sound as she did so, feeling the dirty and delicious nature of her own hand. She speeded up and enjoyed the feeling.

On screen and in the mirror, she was able to watch her own hand as it massaged her clitoris and thrust a finger into her vagina. She was overcome by images of herself and what she was doing. The muscles in her body caved in to the inevitable and she let the first wave of her orgasm rise in her, feeling herself coming and watching herself too.

Her muscles stiffened and she felt her pussy tighten its grip. She stopped moving up and down on it and the only remaining motion was her hand on her clitoris. The room was quiet except for her own groans and whines.

The fluorescent lights reactivated just as the first tremble of her orgasm readied itself and she contracted tightly. She convulsed and shouted out as she came in powerful bursts.

She was demolished by her orgasm. Her desire had created a most delicate and intense construction, full of detail, each peculiarity her own, and now it was being torn down as the raw physical nature of the orgasm shook her to her foundations. In the rush of feelings she had lost her sense of time, her sense of place, even her sense of self. Karen writhed and jolted about, the light burning into her sweaty eyes.

Her breathing returned only gradually to its normal rhythm. She picked up the controller and pressed button number one, the lights dimming as she did so.

Chapter Eight

KAREN FELT EYES on them from every quarter. The stares were not, however, for her. She was having dinner at New York's Gotham Bar and Grill with Jake and a friend of his. It was the fact that the friend was one of the hottest post-Brat Pack actors that was drawing the collective furtive stare.

Chris Nichol, at twenty-seven, had been in several reasonably successful movies, commercially and artistically, and the world seemed poised for his leap to stardom. It would have been pointless to describe him as movie star handsome because that was precisely what he was, but he had none of the menace common to his generation of actors. Instead, he oozed a wholesomeness and down-home politeness and charm, particularly cute when he seemed embarrassed by the attention he was getting.

'You will be in the gossip columns tomorrow, Karen,' Jake said. 'Chris Nichol and mystery date seen on the town with up-and-coming video-maker Jake Summer.'

The contrast between Chris and Jake was so marked, Karen thought. If somebody had asked Karen the question, what is the first thing that springs to mind when someone mentions an English video director living in America, she would have responded, lots of black clothing, and long hair, prematurely greying and tied in a ponytail. Features that were heavy and rubber-like, eyes that were grey and glassy. That was what she would have answered to such a question and that was also what described Jake.

Chris Nichol was at the opposite end of the spectrum and had yet to make the journey Jake wore so obviously in his demeanour. Chris had the collegiate look, a sophomore rather than a freshman, just knowing enough, but not quite spoiled by the knowledge. His hair was short and black, shaped neatly, and his nose was grand, giving him the slightly regal East Coast look he had milked so well in his movies. When he smiled, his face was filled by it, his teeth naturally perfect and his head dropping slightly as though trying to win her over to a point of view or apologising for coming home drunk the night before. He made her feel like they had known each other for a long time.

'This isn't really a glitzy Hollywood place, is it? I've never thought so,' Karen said.

'Glitzy?' Chris repeated. 'I like that word.' He continued to pick away at his dessert, moving impishly, as though he were Karen and Jake's errant son out for his graduation dinner with them. He looked up at her suddenly.

'So Karen,' he asked her, 'do you have a boyfriend back in England?'

'If I remember Karen correctly,' Jake interrupted, 'she will have several. All chasing her and wooing her madly and she just taking her pick.'

'Please. I hardly need to speak with you singing my praises. I'm seeing someone on and off,' she said, directing her last sentence towards Chris.

'More off or more on?' he said.

'Fifty-fifty, I'd say.'

'Hmm,' he grunted, considering this before reconsidering the fruit concoction in front of him.

Jake had privately told Karen that he was wooing Chris Nichol with the hope of attaching him to a film project his production company had in development.

With Chris Nichol attached, the project may just break out of development-hell and get picked up by a studio. Jake had directed several videos for one of Chris's favourite English bands and they had met on the set of one. The two of them seemed to get on well enough and, as far as was possible, lacked the kind of falsity in their friendship Karen would have expected in the movie business.

'Are you seeing anyone back in LA?' she asked, turning his question back at him.

'More off than on. Thirty/seventy, I'd say.' He beamed at her, pleased with himself. If he hadn't been so damn nice, she'd have cut him dead there and then. But she wanted to play a while.

'An ageing starlet?' she asked, raising her brow.

'Over twenty is ageing out there. I make it a rule to try and not fuck actresses,' he said.

'Try and make it a rule. Do you try and succeed?'

'Most of the time,' he replied, chewing on fruit. 'You never jump the customers, I guess, so it's the same, right?'

'Don't assume anything!' Jake interjected loudly. 'Karen could tell you stories and I'm sure she will.'

'Actually Chris, Karen could tell you a lot of stories about Jake,' she said, enjoying referring to herself in third person, 'but I'm sure he wouldn't want me to any more than I would want him to about me.' She shot Jake a glare and he merely smiled, his eyes the colour of smoke.

'I'll get the check,' Jake said eventually, obviously enjoying the repartee. 'But first I have to use the bathroom.' He got up and left.

'He's hoping I'll do this movie for him or just sound like I want to enough to convince a studio to buy it. You know Jake better than I do – what do you think?'

'Well, his videos are wonderful and he's a lovely man to work with once you get past the bullshit. We used him for an in-store video that we showed as a promo and it went over well.'

'I guess, but selling perfume is different to directing a movie. We'll see.'

He looked at her and Karen was aware of him consciously switching on his charisma. She felt it from across the table as though the whole place were suddenly deserted and it was just the two of them. It's just like a movie, she thought, desire rising in her as she looked at him and felt the warmth he exuded. He cracked the smallest of smiles at her and she saw him signal with his eyes. He was not arrogant or even particularly confident, licking his lips slightly as if he wanted to ask her something. Inside, her better judgement tried to win out but she was having little trouble beating it down into a poor second place.

The taxi ride back to Jake's was filled with tension and anticipation for Karen. If Jake had not been there, she wondered if the journey would have ended in a similar way to her last taxi ride in London with Richard. Jake kept the conversation going and everyone joined in the banter, but Chris was interested only in her, she could tell. Jake had not picked up on it and as he burbled on, laughing at himself, Chris would keep his attention on her with a different look in his eyes.

He held her arm to help her out of the taxi and she felt confidence in his grip, their eyes meeting for a frozen moment as she stepped on to the sidewalk, an acknowledgement from each of them of what they wanted. Jake, still unaware, was paying the driver.

The three of them sat in Jake's living-room, sipping wine and mineral water. It was just after eleven-thirty in the evening and Karen was still not in sync with the time-zone, her mind racing and her body following not far behind it. Chris sat on an armchair, legs crossed, and they chatted and laughed. Jake had put on some low music, very jazzy and tasteful and typically Jake.

'So do you go and see many films?' Karen asked Chris.

'Premieres mostly. When I was a kid, I'd cut classes

and go all the time. It was why I wanted to be an actor. Or I went because I knew deep down I wanted to act. I'm not sure which and both sound pretty hokey. You see many movies?'

'Just the big ones or the obscure ones that get recommended. It's a time thing. Jake's probably seen enough films for all of us,' Karen said.

'I have a very filmic imagination, always have,' said Jake. 'Chris, don't you think Karen's pretty enough to have made it in the movies?'

'Of course,' he answered without hesitation. 'Cast her in your movie and you'd have my signature,' he said and Karen saw Jake eye him as though to ask if he were serious. She knew Jake would stop at nothing for that break.

'Would you do a love scene, Karen?' Jake asked her.

Karen felt her temperature rise in the most pleasurable way she knew.

'For the camera you mean? With the right person and the right director, I suppose. Chris must know more about this than either of us,' she said, looking at him.

'It's just like everyone says, really unerotic, lots of people around, lights, worrying about shadows and are you moving in the right way.'

'Would you direct a love scene, Jake?' Karen asked him.

'Of course,' he answered.

'How would you start it?' Chris asked him.

'Two good-looking people in a living room in an apartment in Greenwich Village. They've not really known each other long, but they want to enjoy the sex enough not to just go at it hell for leather the first time. They both want it.'

Jake stood and went to the chair by the small bar in the corner and sat on it, surveying the room in front of him. He casually took a sip from his wine glass and looked at the two of them sitting opposite each other. Karen watched his eyes roving over them like a camera, zooming and focusing. He spoke and his words sounded like the only thing in the room.

'He gets up from his chair and approaches her, very deliberately and carefully, not like he's stalking prey exactly but something close to it, a definite precision to the act. For a moment he stands, towering over her, and she looks up at him. It is a moment of tension but also of the first release of the tension and the transformation of it into something else much more powerful. He crouches and looks at her, their eyes meeting, and he leans over and kisses her passionately.'

Chris's lips were wandering over hers and Karen reciprocated, tasting the wine on his mouth and flicking her tongue at his, the two meeting and touching before darting back. His hair was soft to the touch and bristled on the back of his neck, the muscles there powerful and firm. He pulled away from her and they looked at each other, she taking in the fresh face from the new distance, enjoying the intimacy of it. He licked his lips, the way he had in the restaurant, and she wanted to grab him and crush him into her.

'After they break the first kiss, he feels a little confused, not sure where the desire came from and just a bit afraid of where it might lead him. But he is not in control of himself, because he wants her so badly. She sees this and knows that she is in charge of the situation and can lead it wherever she wants. She can tell him to go away now and he will, or, she can tell him to undress because she wants to see him naked.'

'Undress,' Karen said to him. 'Let me see you.'

Chris stood obediently and began to unbutton his crisp white shirt. Karen saw his long fingers easily untwist the buttons and the shirt come apart from the top down. It was open to the waistband of his trousers and he left it tucked in as he bent down to remove his shoes. Karen saw the hair that covered his chest and ran into a sprinkle over his stomach. The zipper of his trousers sounded loud in the room as he pulled it down, the sound quickly followed by that of his belt undoing. He stepped out of his trousers and discarded them, the white shirt now hanging on him like a nightshirt, held in check by one last button at the bottom which he undid before peeling off the shirt. He stood before her in just jersey grey Calvin Klein boxer shorts, his physique well proportioned and naturally shaped, not too hard and not too soft. He stared at her and then made a face that seemed to say 'what the hell' and put his thumbs in either side of the waistband of the shorts and pushed them over hips, down his legs and off.

'Naked in front of her, he now feels better than he did, like he has nothing to hide from her. This is him. He touches himself, releasing himself and letting his cock hang freely, slowly getting tumescent. He is just going to stand there now and let her make the next move, which she does.'

Karen took in his naked body, the curve and contour of it, the simple manliness of his outline and the gentle hairiness which caught the light and threw strange shadows about him. She sat forward and placed her hands on his hips, cupping him and squeezing lightly to feel the bone beneath. She looked up at him and he was gazing at her, loose in her grip and ready to go wherever she wanted. She slid her hand around and held his behind, which was tight, and then she stood and kissed him with more force than he just had, opening her mouth and allowing him into her. She placed her arms around him and hugged him, almost like he was an old friend she was meeting at a train station. She pulled him tightly, his skin against her clothes, and it excited her and made her want to be naked as well, so that she could get closer to him.

'He is enjoying her touch and the safety it gives him. He can tell that she wants to be undressed as well by the look on her face. He removes himself from the embrace and takes her in, enjoying the vision and the expectation of her nudity, imagining all the while what

84

her body will look like. He sees it in his mind as lithe and hard in all the right places. He will lift her breasts in his hands, weigh up the cheeks of her ass and toy with her pussy, opening it and ravishing it with all he has to offer. But first, he must undress her. He does this silently and with care.'

Karen had long since kicked off her shoes and now stood in her stockinged feet. Chris went down on his haunches and reached up under her dress, pulling off her tights and then quickly following it with her panties. She was surprised that he had gone for them so quickly, imagining that he would leave her in her underwear for a moment in the same way he had been in front of her earlier on. He undid her skirt – the button in the back and the zipper – and it fell to the floor, a pile around her ankles. Karen instantly felt naked even though her top half was still fully clothed. She knew that her blouse was covering her sex so that Chris could not see it, but she still felt as though she were on show. With the buttons on her blouse, he took longer, and when they were undone he pushed the material over her shoulders and let it fall down her back. He turned her around, not even glancing downwards, and unclasped her bra, easing it down her arms with a slinky, dirty motion.

'Now that she's naked and has her back to him, he moves in behind her and lets his cock rest against her behind. He touches her stomach, impressed by the taut flatness of it, and spreads his palms out on her pelvis, pushing her further into him. He leans down and bites her shoulder, making her jump like an electrical current has run through her body. His hand tickles at the nap of her pubic hair and a finger traces down to find the opening, which is moist, hinting at a deeper and more profound wetness. With prudence, he pushes a finger in, barely disturbing the lips but already finding the wetness he knew would be there.'

Just at the opening of her sex, Chris's finger was only the beginning as Karen felt it push in lightly, awakening her inner muscles which had started to jar and jump with excitement. Her breath escaped in long pants and she felt his breath on her shoulder as hot as her own. His cock was nestled against her buttocks and she could feel it expanding, the weight and the heat of it betraying his growing desire to penetrate her with it. She reached around and gripped him, running the head of his cock over the cheeks of her behind and then in between them, he adjusting the position of his legs to allow for maximum stimulation. Her anus trembled as the head of his cock passed over it and she felt her desire take a different direction, one she had seldom charted and now realised she wanted to.

She leaned her head back and pulled his forward, nuzzling his ear and whispering into it. 'Fuck me, please.'

'Waiting for him, she kneels on the sofa and bends forward so that her behind is presented to him in such a way that will make it easy for him to fuck her there. The deep bend of her position on the sofa has spread the cheeks of her behind and just visible is her anus, tight and puckered, but ready to yield to touch and entry. He returns and kneels, kissing her rear and removing the lid from a large jar. He takes a dollop of the clear gel-like substance on one finger and rubs it in the general area of her anus, a prelude to the long and tantalisingly languorous fingering he will give her to ready her for the size of his cock.'

The cream was cold in the first instant it touched her, but Karen soon felt it warm up as the long fingers massaged it around her opening, not venturing in but merely making her ready for the first tentative digit to enter her. The cream made a squelching sound as it was applied to her and the attention she was receiving in this area served to amplify the feeling in her pussy and made her wonder whether she needed to be penetrated there or if she simply needed to be penetrated.

The muscles of her anus were tight around the tip of

his finger as she felt it probe perhaps a half an inch, the sensation more of widening her than entering her. The skin on his finger was lined and she was sure she could feel the outline of his fingerprints against the slicked and smooth skin of her anal passage. A tiny mound of cream was placed directly over her entrance and then his finger suddenly pushed into her, taking the cream with it as it went up into her. As quickly as it had been there, so the finger was withdrawn. Karen fidgeted with her knees while all the time her behind cried out for more attention now that it had been inflamed by the gentlest of touches.

'For a while, he just stops and looks at her crouched on the sofa and on show for him. He thinks about the restaurant earlier and the way he had desired her then, wondering if he would be able to fuck her. Now, he can't believe his luck. Here she is, pushing her ass up in the air and asking him to fuck it. Her body turns him on, the position of it. His cock is hard and painful and soon he will slick it up with the same gel he has been using on her and they will become one.'

The first stage of the fingering was very coy, shy almost, and Karen could imagine it as an extension of the persona Chris had exuded in the restaurant. The innocence and the freshness, the naivety and the willingness to learn. He was a fast learner. Soon he had two fingers pushed into her, all the way up to the knuckles, and he worked away at her with a gradually increasing speed. He stopped and slopped an enormous amount of the lubricant on to her, as though she were being flooded, and this time she felt him go to work with a third finger slowly entering the fray. He began by just using the two, which her anus had now relaxed and expanded enough to accommodate, and then she felt the third finger push at her as the two came out and made the downward plunge. He slowed the fingering and decreased its depth, concentrating more on getting the third finger into her. They pushed against her anus and she relished the feeling, the way she would comply with his intrusion only for him to increase its scale. Karen relaxed herself, pushed back on to his hand and, with a slippery shove, he had three fingers inside her.

'He has three fingers in her now and can feel her warming up and becoming loose enough for him to be able to fuck her. He thinks about putting in his little finger as well and then resting his thumb on her ass while the rest of his hand casually fucks her brains out, but he thinks better of it. Instead, he'll keep on at her for a while longer, getting her ready for him and ready to accept him into her. He listens to the sound of her breathing and the noises she is making, wondering if she is even aware of her own sounds or if she is utterly lost, astray in her own passion.'

Empty of his fingers, Karen gaped and puckered, her rear end a warm and greasy combination of tension and relaxation, ready to be pushed further. She heard him work the gel on to himself and looked behind her to watch him, his face a study of concentration which made him look even prettier and cuter. Here he was, the college boy adorning the walls of teenage bedrooms, about to take her from behind. She quivered at the prospect and played her fingers over her clitoris, shocked by the wetness there and the sensitivity of her bud. She heard him approach her.

It was much wider than even his three fingers. The fingers had been more moveable and free in her, whereas his cock was wide and solid, able only to plough a single furrow into her without by or leave. The advance of it into her was relentless as it forged a path into her well-prepared rear. Just when she thought she was full, so Chris eased himself still further, holding the cheeks of her behind and splaying them. His balls came to rest against her oiled buttocks and she was glad that this part of it was over.

'He's deep inside her now, feeling a part of her and feeling not a part of her. Both alien and native. He enjoys the feel of her ass against his pubic hair and the way his cock looks stuffed into her, the ring of her anus holding on to his shaft. He reaches down and pushes a finger on the top of his shaft and manages to get it into her a short way, making her cry out. He likes the feel the finger makes on his own cock and leaves it there for a while. His balls feel heavy with come and his cock stifled by the blood that has gushed into it in the preceding moments. What he wants now, at this moment, is very simple, despite the deeper complexities of sex. He wants simply to fuck her.'

Karen's whole rear moved with the motion of his thrusts. Where the fingering had been a preparatory and teasing experience, this was a definite and concentrated effort that she felt was designed to bring both of them off as quickly as possible. The depth, speed and intensity of his drives into her all indicated this. She was pushed into the soft cushions of the sofa by his energy and his hands were on her hips, using them like handles with which to control the speed of something that would ultimately become uncontrollable. His hips made a slapping sound as they made contact with her behind, finishing with a thud as his cock rammed home.

The pace was now frantic and Chris was murmuring and mumbling to himself although Karen could not tell what he was saying. It sounded like he was coaxing and egging himself on, wanting to continue fucking her for as long as possible but unable to resist the urge to let it spill over and end. Carefully, Karen massaged her clitoris and used the feelings of her rear as a focal point for the pleasure that was about to soak through her. The whole region below, both her pussy and her anus, were alive and involved in the heat of the fucking.

He gasped and his legs seemed to tremble and his whole body spin out of control, like a fighter plane that had been shot down and was in a frantic tailspin. The act of fucking her which had been initiated by him seemed to have become bigger than him and was now in control of him rather than the other way around. His passion built and swelled like a wave in Karen and she was ready to ride it. As he shouted and she felt his cock pulsate, she came in brief and throbbing spasms, the walls of her vagina rippling around nothing, the muscle of her anus echoing its motions and finding the thick cock there. Warm shots of semen filled her and she slumped forward on the sofa, her face twisted by the exertion of her orgasm. She shook and convulsed, grinding her rear on to him and squeezing his cock with it as it gushed forth into her.

With cries and gasps of almost identical pitch and length, they were finished.

'Cut.'

Chapter Nine

NEW YORK HAD gone, and felt, like a dream.

As far as going like a dream, Karen had met with several people, her usual contacts and some they had in turn introduced her to, and these meetings produced useful discussions about Hamiltons in general and The Garden in particular. She had picked up some ideas and was formulating them into her original thoughts, ready to pitch it at Avendon properly. She would call on Alan for help, giving the proposal a firm and solid foundation, and also getting his tacit approval for The Garden as it would help convince Avendon. Karen was not certain Avendon was behind the idea. She believed he may have been paying her some clumsy lip service as a way of apologising for his half-sister's behaviour, although that would have been an unusually magnanimous gesture from him.

New York felt like a dream for quite different reasons, most of them to do with Jake. She was not now sure if she had really seen Maxwell on the video screens in Jake's apartment or if she had simply imagined him as a way of fulfilling a wish deep inside her. Perhaps she had imagined the whole room. She had not mentioned it to Jake nor he to her, so she could not be sure. Chris Nichol, she had not imagined. That was an experience that would remain vivid in her memory for a long time to come, along with the filmic record of what they had done afterwards.

The taxi she had jumped in at Heathrow made the right turn into Sloane Street and she looked through the window, feeling at home and glad to be there, the friendly yellow glow from the shop fronts of Harvey Nichols and YSL Rive Gauche seeming somehow more English than the shop windows of New York, despite the similarity in style between the countries. She was wearing a simple, short Betty Jackson dress with chiffon arms, something she had picked up in Bergdorf Goodman, unable to resist. She had topped it off with a purchase at Saks, a Sonia Rykiel jacket, black with a velour collar and round gold buttons. She had also been through the doors of, and exited with bags from, Henri Bendel, Lord & Taylor and Bloomingdale's. As ever, Macy's was simply too overwhelming to make a purchase there and she had instead wandered around it for almost three hours, still feeling as if she had only scratched the surface.

She paid the driver, tipping and getting a receipt, and gathered her luggage, which had increased considerably since her departure four days earlier. It was just after four in the afternoon and she approached the entrance to her building, looking forward to a shower and some sleep.

'Karen,' said a small mousy voice from behind her.

She knew, as soon as she heard the voice, who it was and was surprised that when David had mentioned the phone messages from the person with the mousy voice a week ago, she had not realised who it would be.

'Caroline,' she said, turning.

'Hi,' said Caroline, her facial muscles weakening and looking ready to break into a sob at any moment.

Karen hugged her and kissed her.

'How have you been? It's been ages. Three months? Six?' Karen asked, the surprise still in her voice.

'Oh, six I think. You know,' she replied, shrugging and widening her eyes at the same time. 'It's been the usual, only worse.'

'Gareth?'

'Oh Karen,' Caroline said, rushing back to hug her again, a small sob going through her.

'You'd better come in,' said Karen.

'So when did you find out?' Karen asked her.

'A month ago, really. He said he had to go away on business for two weeks in Hong Kong. I offered to go visit him, but he told me there wouldn't be any time, meetings everyday and that it wouldn't look good if he took his girlfriend out there.'

Caroline was speaking quickly, sniffling and sipping from a cup of tea.

Karen had known Caroline since they were in the same halls of residence at university. They were the same age, but Caroline could have been her mother or her little sister, depending on how life was choosing to treat her at any given moment. Right now, it was dealing her a pretty lousy hand. Karen had only met Gareth twice. Once had been enough, but she had stretched to a second time for the sake of her friend. He was exactly what Karen imagined when someone used the word prat. A loud, obvious, overgrown and brash rugby-playing boor would have been another description.

'But didn't you suspect something before that?' Karen asked.

'Sort of. Not really. Yes. I thought he was just busy at work, which was why I saw so little of him and that when I did, he was too tired from all the work. And I thought a bit of the shine went out when I moved in with him and that it would probably get better. Just that the idea of living with someone scared him – the commitment, you know.'

'I thought Gareth's idea of commitment was talking to you after he'd come,' Karen said, regretting it as soon as the words were out.

'Karen, I know you thought he was an arsehole, but

I loved him. I still do,' she snivelled again, hiding it in the cup of tea.

Karen sighed. What was she supposed to say? You could never be honest with your friends about their choice of partners while they were still with them – that would be dangerous. She looked at Caroline and thought of some of the bastards she had hooked up with at university – the evenings Caroline had spent fretting about them, the days Caroline had been depressed, and all for someone Karen would not have bothered even to give the brush-off to. Not a lot had changed for Caroline, she thought.

Caroline could only be described as almost. For as long as Karen had known her, Caroline's hair was almost right, her dress sense almost right and her personality almost right. But not quite. It frustrated Karen that Caroline was so close to being an attractive and interesting person but seemed incapable of the short journey to the point where she actually was. Karen had tried to drag her there on numerous occasions, offering to help her with clothes, to fix her hair and just to push herself a bit more. None of this had ever worked and Caroline seemed to drift from job to job, flat to flat and man to man, never quite settling. Almost, but never quite.

Karen had thought that Gareth had changed that. Caroline had been seeing him for nearly a year and he had suggested to her that she move in. Caroline had been excited at the time and Karen tried to share it, but she had diminished her contact with Caroline mostly because of Gareth. She was suspicious about him and his motives concerning Caroline. When she was first introduced to him, Karen felt his eyes rove over her lasciviously and she knew instantly the sort of man he would be. Certainly not the sort for Caroline. After that, she had seen Caroline alone for girls' nights out, but Gareth on only one other occasion and then he had been frosty to her.

Caroline sat on the sofa, sipping tea, pushing her

hand through her dirty blonde hair and frowning through her clumsy make-up. Karen knew that she should offer to let her stay and was prepared to, but was not sure if she wanted to do the guardian angel bit right at that moment, particularly with the work The Garden would involve in the coming weeks. Caroline had regained her composure and now seemed to be a bit angry at Gareth, which made the tale more lucid.

'She's some cow he used to see at work. She left the company and went to work for a competitor. Her name's Marilyn. He actually called me it once and tried to make me think I hadn't heard him properly and that he'd really said Caroline.' She shook her head, recalling her past foolishness. Karen smiled sympathetically.

'How did you find out exactly?'

'She sent him this card, a crude one about a pussy eating a cock, and I found it. Gareth just thought I wouldn't find it. He can be so stupid. Or perhaps he wanted me to find it, I don't know. Perhaps. When I did find it, I went mad. He told me she was pestering him, tried to paint it like *Fatal Attraction* or something.'

'When did all this happen?' Karen asked her friend.

'Three weeks ago, just before this supposed Hong Kong trip. He'd been telling me about this trip for two months and there was no way he wasn't going to go, just because of me. That's what he told me, like it was my fault. I found the name of her company and called her last week. She's away on holiday for three weeks. Then I called Gareth's company, using a funny voice – I must be mad. He's away on holiday. Not business, but a holiday.' She sniffed.

'Have you left him?'

'As good as. I'm going to sort a place out while he's away and then move my stuff into it. I've left the temping job I was doing and I hope I can just put him out of my mind and my life by the time he gets back.'

Mentally, Karen ran a hand through her own hair and shrugged and sighed; it was so like Caroline to give up her temporary job just when she would most need her independence.

'You know you can stay here if you need to. There's room. When is he due back?'

'A week next Tuesday. Are you sure it's not a pain? You're the best person I could think of.'

'Borrow some of my clothes for tonight and tomorrow night we'll go and pick up your stuff and store it here. I'd do it now, but I just got back from a trip and I'm exhausted,' Karen said, suddenly feeling weary.

'Your assistant told me you were in New York. He got quite stroppy about me not leaving my name.'

'You've been haunting him for the last three weeks,' Karen said. 'He wants to find out who you are.'

'You can tell him he's got a very sexy voice,' Caroline said, brightening a little.

'I hate to be the one to tell you but . . .'

'Gay?' Caroline interjected before Karen could finish the sentence.

Karen nodded solemnly and they both burst into laughter that they held on to and let subside into a few moments of silence.

'Karen, I'm so rude. How are you? I haven't even asked.'

'Same as I ever was. Busy.'

'What exciting promotions have you done lately? I keep an eye out for advertisements.'

'The current one is a bit different,' Karen said. 'Hamiltons are launching a unisex fragrance and I convinced them that I could handle the creative side of the advertising campaign.'

'That was clever.'

'Thank you. There's minimal risk as the launch is quite low-key. We're not looking to shift a million units in the first month. Linda Cole is doing the photography for us.'

'Linda? I haven't spoken to her in ages. How is she?'

'She's doing great as far as I can tell. She's become

more of a business acquaintance these days,' Karen told her.

'You two were so close at college. The bad girls.'

'She's still bad. She's seeing a model. Maxwell – do you know who I mean?'

Caroline pondered the name for a moment. 'The boy who was in that advert for mineral water?'

'Yes,' Karen said, having partly forgotten the commercial.

'That sounds like Linda.'

'We're using him as a model for the campaign. He's adorable. I could use him for a few things,' she said.

'How's Daniel? Still oddball?'

'Very,' she said. 'Some half-sister of his has crawled out of the woodwork and there are rumours flying around the shop about why she's here. She has a stake in the shop and could cause trouble. She used to work in the shop and I've already heard a story about her poking her nose into something. We'll see.'

'Are you seeing anyone?' Caroline asked, a glint in her eye.

'More than just one. Two, actually and it's getting very awkward.'

'Karen! Who?'

'They both work at Hamiltons. One's younger than me and the other one's older – quite a bit older in fact.'

'Do they know about each other?'

'No! That's why it's getting difficult, being in two places at once.'

'Do you have a favourite? The older one, I bet?'

'You know me, I've never really weighed or measured those sort of things, but now it seems like I have to. Stringing them both along doesn't seem to be a choice.'

'What would happen if you came clean with them?'

'The younger one, Richard, would be all right about it, I know that. We're pretty free with each other. The older one is more difficult. He's just been through a bad divorce. I don't want him to think I've let him down.'

'And I bet you're still getting into the odd tussle, aren't you?' Caroline said.

The word tussle had become a kind of code for them to signify Karen's occasional forays, her seizing of opportunities.

'One or two,' she replied modestly.

'You're still searching, Karen, aren't you? I thought I'd stopped and that the search was over with Gareth. Turns out I was just off the scent for a while.'

'Like he was a hunt saboteur, you mean?' Karen said.

'Something like that.'

They wiled away almost two hours, remembering their times at university, friends and enemies, things they would have done differently, things they were glad they had done. Karen realised that she had missed Caroline without noticing it consciously and she was glad to see her again. Somewhere during the conversation she put on a record she had not heard for ages and for a while was transported, regressing almost, as she and Caroline shamelessly reminisced about who they used to be. Eventually the jet-lag got the better of Karen and she had a quick shower and showed Caroline where things were before she turned in, just before nine. She called Richard and arranged to see him in the shop first thing in the morning, knowing she would be up early. As she drifted off to sleep, she made a mental note to try and find Caroline some work at Hamiltons.

In her own bed, between the pure linen sheets, she drifted through multiple video images of doves and falcons, hooded in the sunset and coming to transport her to the garden.

Chapter Ten

KAREN ENTERED HAMILTONS through the special side entrance, exchanging pleasantries with the guard as she signed in. It was ten minutes before seven in the morning. Richard had signed in fifteen minutes earlier and she knew exactly where she would find him.

The menswear department was described by everyone in Hamiltons as The Dungeon. The room was square and the main access, certainly as far as customers were concerned, was down a wide and dramatic staircase that felt like a descent into Hell. The stairs were a granite material with heavy welts and scars cut into them. The air-conditioning was fabulous and the area always had a slight chill to it. With its menswear, unlike the womens', Hamiltons went for the younger, high-spending and fashion-conscious end of the market. There were no good old trusty names in the dungeon. No Chester Barrie, Aquascutum or Jaeger. One such designer had once actually persuaded Daniel Avendon to model one of his suits. Daniel beamed out and beneath him a caption read, 'When it comes to menswear, even he has to go elsewhere.'

The department was laid out in a way that tried to fuse styles. Rather than have areas dedicated to a single designer, ranges would be blended in an attempt to create a look. Karen always had trouble every time they ran a promotion connected with menswear. They were successful promotions but setting them up was difficult as it meant trying to deal with the primadonnas who staffed the area. The most recent promotion for boxer shorts had gone better than anyone expected, but the dungeon staff still thought they could do it better than her.

Gently, she took the steps one at a time, hardly making a sound. She smiled when she saw Richard, unaware of her and trying on a jacket, turning and looking at himself, flicking his hair out of his eyes and jutting his chin forward. Karen found him vain in the sweetest possible way, his adorable face, even with his squarish nose, making her forgive whatever he did. He took the jacket off, replacing it on the hanger and preening it before returning it to the rail, then picking another, much more garish one. The bright yellow check set against his honey-coloured skin and this time he let his hair fall forward into his eyes. Becoming aware of her presence, he turned, completely unflustered and unembarrassed, and launched a smile that grew over his face with disarming rapidity. Karen realised that she had missed him while she was in New York.

'How long were you watching me?' he asked her.

'Oh, ages and ages. Me and all the guards on the cameras I expect.' She scooped his face up in her hands and kissed him directly on the mouth, comforted by the familiarity and intimacy.

'I've missed you, I really have,' she said to him warmly.

'You sound surprised. This is nice,' he said, looking at her outfit. 'It's not like you to wear Gucci.'

'Show-off,' she said.

'How was New York? Did they have the new Calvin Klein yet?'

From her pocket, in a well prepared and practised motion, she produced a bottle of eau de toilette from the new Calvin Klein range, not due for launch in the UK for another six months. He scrabbled the cellophane off, tore the box open and quickly sprayed it into the air. A flowery smell soon rose in the dungeon.

'It's brilliant. Did you pay full price for it?'

'Of course not. What have you been up to while I was away?'

'Nothing much. Same old same old. You know.'

'I was going to call but I was busy,' she said, wishing she had phoned him after she had called Alan on the second evening.

'How do I look in this?' he asked her, shrugging his shoulders and allowing the jacket to fall and move around his broad frame.

'Not as good as you'd look out of it,' she said to him.

'Is this why we're here so early?'

'I was too tired last night and I really wanted to see you. Do you mind if we go up to the furniture department?'

'You want to do it in the furniture department? The guards will enjoy that.'

'No, it's business. I wanted to look at it before anyone arrived. Then we can go to my office or even to the flat. No security cameras there,' she said.

'I wonder if they bug your office?'

'I hope so.'

They went up the granite steps and took the ground-floor lift to the fourth floor. The furniture department occupied several thousand square feet. Karen tried to visualise The Garden fitting somewhere into it. There had been talk of contracting the space the furniture section occupied for some time. It was Hamiltons' least profitable line of business and took up too much space relative to the profit it generated, staying largely because no one knew what to put in its place. Karen hoped she had found the solution to that problem.

'Are you looking at anything in particular?' Richard asked her.

'No. I just wanted to see something. Come here,

you,' she said, pulling him towards her and then spinning him so his back was against a large and ornate fitted wardrobe. Here she repeated the earlier kiss, but with a greater depth and intensity. They were in a quiet corner away from the prying eyes of the store cameras, of which there were less in the furniture department, stealing being that much more difficult.

Richard's hair was tousled and falling over his forehead in spindly strands as she pushed and pulled at him, unsure of exactly what she wanted to do with him. She was just roughing him up a little, running her hands over his trousers – which he had already told her were Bill Blass – gripping the bits of him that protruded, feeling her way round his body, reintroducing herself to him and his essence, the smell, touch and taste of him. He was responding in kind, his hands inside her jacket and then on her hips. He was erect and his cock pushed against her. She shoved him harder against the wardrobe, feeling the dull thud his body made.

'I still owe you for that taxi ride,' she said.

'More of a joy ride, wasn't it?' he said naughtily.

Karen fumbled at the zip of his trousers, and the slow tearing sound it made as she pulled it down sent a shiver through her. His underwear pushed out of the fly from the pressure of his cock. He had placed his hands on her shoulders, surrendering all control to her, and she reached down and carefully removed him from the fly, slipping it through a similar fly in his boxer shorts. As he stood, fully clothed but with his long and erect cock sticking out of his trousers, Karen wanted practically to attack him, barely knowing where to start first, her passion for him multiplied by her absence of just a few days.

Dropping to her knees, she smothered him with her mouth, her lips quickly coming against the fabric of his trousers. They had never really had sex in the morning as much as she would have liked and Karen was pleased to discover that he was a morning person as

102

well as a night-time one. With her tongue, she sent signals to him, flicking herself against his shaft and over the head, skilfully rolling over the ridge of his phallus and then under to the glans which she burrowed into. Richard's hands stayed on her shoulders but his grip tightened, the beginnings of movement stirring in his groin, Karen's mouth relaxing and stretching to accommodate all of him that was on offer through the small gap in his fly.

Pulling him from her mouth, Karen licked frantically at his shaft, smearing him before swallowing him up again, the acid of his fluid on her tongue. She placed both hands on his hips and increased the speed with which she took him in and out of her mouth and he sighed, his hands roving over her shoulders and into the hair at the back of her neck.

'. . . do something about this area here.'

Karen stopped, thinking Richard had said something, but unsure through the wet noises she had been making on him with her mouth. She felt his body stiffen and she looked up at him.

'Someone's coming,' he whispered harshly.

'We could move some of the beds out, open the floor up a bit,' a voice was saying.

Karen stood up quickly, the voices almost upon them, sounding about to round the corner into their no longer so private cranny. As quickly as she could whilst being silent, Karen opened the door of the wardrobe and pushed Richard into it, following him then closing it.

In the darkness, she could hear him panting, sucking in lots of air and trying to regulate and silence himself. Karen was a mix of arousal and adrenalin. They were completely in the dark, the tight space of the wardrobe allowing no light in. Karen listened, but the voices were muffled, the wardrobe affording a reasonable degree of soundproofing.

'What should we do?' he whispered, his body pressed up behind her.

Karen reached behind and found what she was looking for. In the warm darkness of the wardrobe, beneath the sounds of muffled voices from outside, she manipulated Richard's cock until the blood began to flow back into it and the shaft became stiff in her hand.

'Not in here?' he said, a slight tremble in his voice.

Richard's cock was hard and with her hand behind her and firmly on him, she moved it up and down, masturbating him awkwardly but effectively nonetheless. Carefully and with his arms gently knocking the wardrobe, he hitched up her skirt and pushed her knickers down as far as he could given his restricted movement. With her panties around her knees, she released her hold on his cock and allowed him to explore her crotch under the front of her dress.

His hands roamed, stroking and brushing her skin in the sensitive area of her groin, the palms of his hands slightly coarse on the satiny skin it explored. Karen left him to it, happy for him to forage around in the darkness of the wardrobe and the darker depths of her. He circled the tops of her thighs, drawing nearer to the tops of her legs and the crevice between them, his fingers imploring and her pussy equally willing.

Despite the darkness, Karen still clenched her eyes tightly shut when he dipped a finger into her, the flat of his hand on her pubic hair and his digit confident and driving. She caught her breath, savouring the feel of his finger in her and his cock driving against her behind. Moving her legs, she felt the constriction of her knickers around her knees, preventing what little movement the walls of the wardrobe would have afforded. She realised that she would have to make her pleasure with what was available, moving her body in the small space around her, manipulating the both of them with care. She pressed herself against one of the side walls, the muffled voices on the outside long-forgotten, and arched her backside to him, making the angle of her pussy more sheer. He followed her movement with a deft one from his hand and increased the depth of his intrusion into her, his breath feverish against her neck.

While he continued to finger her, she made herself ready, manoeuvring herself into exactly the right position, communicating her desire to him through her actions alone, unable to see him, this presence in the darkness that fingered her with a relentlessness both brutal and compassionate. Her juices coursed around his fingers, a sucking sound coming from the combination of hand and pussy. She bent forward, almost sitting in his lap as he craned his arms around her and continued to push into her and flick at her clit with his thumb.

Karen moved away from him and reached around to find his member. It was hot in her hand, the flesh slightly damp from the heat their bodies had generated in the confines of the wardrobe. She squeezed it, feeling the way the shaft gave way ever so slightly under her hand, and imagined it buried inside her, rending her pussy-lips apart and filling her. He had stopped fingering her and lifted her skirt up, exposing her behind. Karen guided his cock and rubbed the head of it over the cheeks of her rear, feeling the sticky come glazing over her buttocks. His hand was on hers, gently pushing it off his cock so that he could do the work for her. She put her hands up to allow him free rein and she found the rail that ran across the top of the wardrobe. She gripped on to it, the metal cold under her hands, and suspended herself there as Richard continued to explore her with the tip of his cock.

Along the join of her buttocks and down to the opening of her pussy, Richard investigated her, his cock rigid against her, pushing into the sensitive area between her anus and her pussy, tickling her with a light touch and then returning for a heavier stroke, an indication of what was to come. Karen was still wet from the fingering he had given her and she was ready for him to enter her, to take her carefully from behind in the unlit interior of a wardrobe as she clung, hands above head, to a metal rail. It was as though her whole body had been blindfolded, the remaining senses accentuated – the smell, touch, sound and taste they created between them all flooding through and making up for the loss of vision.

Cautiously and precisely, Karen felt Richard guide his cock into her pussy, nudging at the folds of skin that protected her before they slowly yielded to the thrust and accepted him. The opening of her vagina enlarged with him, expanding to accept his size but holding him tightly enough to make the sensation a precious cross between pain and pleasure. Their posture made it hard for him to get very far into her but Karen found it all the more enticing: once again the space was dictating how they would make their pleasure and she was determined to make the most of it. She let a hand drop from the rail, feeling behind herself, finding where he was in her. She began to move.

Karen rocked tenderly back and forth on to his cock, a gentle and tantalising rhythm, feeling it open and close her and stretch her with each partial entrance. They made few movements, the smell of their bodies all around them and the secret noises of passion amplified and echoing around the tiny cavern. She held on to the rail again, her arms above her head as she backed on to him, feeling the lap of his trousers contacting with her bottom and the rumpled skirt in the small of her back. The end of his cock continued to nudge at the opening of her sex, and Karen arched her back, pushing her pussy out at him to allow his shaft to stab at her clitoris.

The heat of the wardrobe seemed to swell her clitoris and she felt about to erupt into orgasm, hanging off the rail and impaling herself on his unseen rod. He brought his hand around and pressed at her clit, but she needed little stimulation and savoured the closeness of her climax as she continued to keep the same pace to her movements. She was not going to allow herself, or Richard, the luxury of a fast and furious orgasm. She was controlling her movements in order to coax the biggest response she could, from him and her.

'Oh my God,' she heard him whisper, his clutch on her tightening.

His body bobbed up slightly behind her, sending his cock up at her slightly further, and he shuddered.

'Hold it for just a little longer,' she said before dropping her head down.

Still she continued with the relentless and steady movement of her body on to his cock. The first spasm went off between her legs and she drooped, her weight hanging from the rail. As the second wave took hold, she pulled herself back up, the physical reaction now taut rather than loose. In a steady stream of pulsations in time with the methodical movements, she came, the force of it sending the blood rushing around her body. She forgot where she was – the darkness, the heat and the musky odour – as she rode Richard's cock. She was enjoying rearing on to it in the dark as it discharged into her, this stiff cock poking through the fly of his trousers.

For several moments, she clung to the rail. He moved and allowed his cock to slip from her, reaching down and pulling her knickers back up. She heard him do up his fly and then the sound of him running his hands through his hair. She pushed the door a fraction and it clicked open. She listened through the crack and heard nothing.

'I'll go first. You wait for a minute,' she said, deciding to take the chance.

She pushed the door open and walked into the light, blinking and rubbing her eyes as though she had entered another world.

Chapter Eleven

IN THE MEDIUM-SIZED meeting room on the fifth floor of Hamiltons sat Daniel Avendon, his half-sister Gabrielle, Alan Saxton and Karen. The room had two doors, one that led from the corridor outside and the other which was attached to Daniel Avendon's office, causing him to refer to it as his 'en suite' meeting room. Avendon and Gabrielle had just arrived and there was an awkward silence in the air, brought on by Gabrielle's presence.

Fifteen minutes earlier, Karen had been in Alan's office discussing the proposal she had put together for The Garden. Alan had been extremely helpful and Karen was confident that Avendon would be sufficiently impressed to give the go-ahead. Alan had assured her that there was no way Daniel would bring Gabrielle along to the meeting. Obviously, Alan had been wrong and Karen looked across at him, he returning the gaze with an expression that said little. Part of her had been ready for it. David had given her the full story about how Gabrielle had tried to stop one of the buyers in the china department making a routine purchase and the drama that had followed. The management at Hamiltons were awaiting some kind of announcement regarding Gabrielle. What her role in Hamiltons was to be, if any. Based on her first interaction with her in Daniel's office and on the stories that were going round, Karen knew full well that Gabrielle would be attending the meeting. Karen even had four copies of the proposal prepared in case it happened. She was not going to change her basic pitch, whatever the circumstances, because she believed in it and in its ability to sell itself.

They exchanged some pleasantries, Gabrielle as distant and aloof as she had been the first time Karen met her, and then they got down to the purpose of the meeting – to discuss The Garden. Karen handed each of them a copy of the proposal, which was bound in a clear plastic cover, the image of a snake slithering across the bottom right corner of the title page. She watched Daniel's face as he scanned the proposal, leafing through. Gabrielle did not even pick it up. Alan studied it courteously, having already seen it at least a dozen times in the preparation stage.

'Tell me more,' Avendon said, dropping the proposal on the table and fixing her with a stare.

'A shopping paradise for women,' Karen began. 'An Eden without Adam and a place where no fruit is forbidden. There are,' she continued, 'four levels to The Garden.'

'It's going to be on four floors?' Gabrielle cut in.

Karen gave her the briefest and sharpest look of disdain she felt she could get away with and continued, refusing to let her stride be broken.

'Theory, concept, environment and product. Four levels. Simple.' The last word was directed mainly at Gabrielle.

Avendon nodded thoughtfully, the high-concept stuff appealing to him, and Karen took it as a sign to continue.

'The key to The Garden is choice. It is about women making choices, and it's fun and satisfying. The high theory, if you like, is choice or the freedom to choose.' Karen looked at Gabrielle and Alan, neither of whom seemed entirely convinced. She knew Alan had a predilection for numbers and had heard a lot of this before, so Karen was not surprised by his non-committal look but she wondered where Gabrielle's mind was. Daniel, by contrast, looked keen, his smart features all standing to attention, and appeared interested.

'Concept is the next level. What particular concepts are important?' she asked rhetorically and followed quickly with an answer in case Gabrielle had some stupid comment to make. 'Atmosphere, space and privacy. Hamiltons already has such a wonderful atmosphere and it will be an extension of that. A sub-set dedicated to women. We already get a mix of customers, but The Garden will be for the female. The space needs to be carefully constructed. Practically, we'll locate it in a small area and this will create privacy and comfort.'

Alan was raising his eyebrow and looking interested, as was Avendon. Gabrielle was looking around the room, appearing to study some of the art that adorned its walls.

'The environment. This has specifics.' Karen was even and relaxed in her tone, confident but not over-rehearsed. 'Music but not muzak. Decor should be entertaining, but still tasteful. It's not going to look like one of those tacky gift stores in Oxford Street. Naturally, it will be verdant and garden-like, but in a sexy and earthy way. Service. This is a case of finding the right people, and notice I say *people*, not women or men. There needs to be a definite *type* of person, not the usual Saturday crowd. I want people who are educated and personable.

'All of this,' she continued towards the final point, 'theory, concept and environment, has to play out into one thing. It has to facilitate product. It's a conduit. We're not making any bold statements about femininity here. Hamiltons is not political in that way. We pick a few product lines and put them exclusively in The Garden. Clothes, beauty and accessories form the core – a favourite trinity – and we populate from there with whatever we think fits best. There are a number of suggestions in the proposal.

'It's simple and it's straightforward,' she finished. 'From theory, through concept and environment and on ultimately to product. The basic philosophy of shopping for women only. The Eden without the Adam.'

Karen had finished.

'It will never work.'

It was Gabrielle, suddenly focused in on the conversation and looking directly at Daniel Avendon when she spoke, the now familiar triumphal smile on her face. She was wearing a gown of crushed velvet, a kind of deep mauve colour, that was far too tight for her. Her stomach pressed on the dress and Karen thought she looked like an aubergine. If only her rinse had been a shade more green.

'I will make it work,' Karen said, looking at her and then Avendon. 'What makes you think it won't work?'

'The cost will be far too high,' Gabrielle replied.

'Alan and I have produced detailed costings and see a payback period of just nine months. This is based on a very modest assumption of turnover increase. This is not going to be expensive.' Karen saw Gabrielle take the words in and then ignore them. It must have been obvious to her that Karen knew what she was talking about. Perhaps she wasn't expecting that, Karen thought.

'But who would come to such a department?' Gabrielle said, appearing to change her direction away from the financial aspects. 'Feminists? Lesbians?'

Karen sighed. 'Women will come. Women who already come to Hamiltons and women who have never been to Hamiltons. Women who come for one specific thing will use The Garden to buy others. It's a long-standing promotion, basically.'

'How long would it take to be up and running?' This was Avendon.

'Two months,' Karen replied immediately. 'We can use the back half of the furniture department, sealed off and accessible by a single lift.'

'Two months!' Gabrielle interjected, snorting as she did so.

'I don't know how much Daniel has told you, Gabrielle,' Karen said, turning on her, 'but I have been responsible for some of the most successful promotions this store has ever run. In all its long history. It can be open in two months and after six we will know whether or not it is going to pay off.'

'Alan, what do you think?' Avendon asked.

Alan had been looking at Gabrielle and jumped to attention when Daniel spoke. He paused briefly, in a way familiar to Karen, before embarking on a considered answer.

'Well Daniel, financially it is sound. All we are doing in effect is re-modelling the way we offer some of our products and giving it a different approach. What Karen just called a conduit. The main expense is environmental, but Karen has looked into all of that quite thoroughly and the costs listed here have some leeway.'

'What do you think of it commercially?' Avendon asked him.

'It's not really my field, but I like it. I can see something in it.'

'Don't you think it's a little, well, insulting?' Gabrielle asked. 'Defining us by clothes and lipsticks?'

Karen was about to ask when Gabrielle had suddenly joined the sisterhood but held her tongue.

'There's no statement,' she said instead. 'I've already said that. Hamiltons has always left that up to its customers. They'll take what they want from it.'

'But men will feel excluded,' Gabrielle said, sounding childish.

'Probably,' Karen replied.

'Karen, how many people will it need?' asked Daniel.

'Alan and I think twenty-five to thirty staff, including five supervisors over teams of four. Every team should have full knowledge of the product-offering in The Garden. We can re-deploy at least ten people from in-house and the rest we could take on temp to perm six-month contracts.'

Karen looked over at Alan and he gave her an encouraging smile with one side of his mouth.

'Advertising?' said Avendon.

'We restrict it to a few good magazines – *Vanity Fair*, *Tatler*, *Cosmo* and maybe *Marie Claire*, but no lower than that,' Karen said.

'Talk me through The Garden,' Avendon said dreamily. 'I am a woman and I've just arrived at Hamiltons.'

'You will be able to get to it only by a lift from the ground floor,' said Karen. 'One or two people will act as greeters on the ground floor. The inside of the lift will have pictures of famous women, some of the Hamiltons library ones from the Fifties where they're actually in the store. Elizabeth Taylor, Lauren Bacall, Joan Fontaine, Vivien Leigh. A few notable quotes. Some announcements in the lift about what to expect in The Garden, the need to ask if you want assistance, that sort of thing.

'When the lift arrives and the doors open, your world will change. It will knock you over. The lighting will be artificial, creating a perpetual but gentle daylight and the surroundings will be lush and green with foliage but it will not be like a jungle or a greenhouse. The atmosphere will be pleasantly cool, a sound of water in the background. The colouring will be differing shades of green, very relaxing. No more greeters. You'll be on your own from there. People will be on hand to help if you ask, but you won't be mugged like when you walk into Gap.'

'You'll be able to wander freely around a select range of cosmetics, the new Hamiltons fragrance at centre stage. Lingerie, hats, clothes, bags and shoes. All the best of Hamiltons will be distilled and captured and it will be there for you. A bar will serve complimentary juices and there will be plenty of sofas for you to relax on and read the various magazines.

'From start to finish, the experience should be easy and lacking in pressure. And, importantly, all the other customers will be women and the whole concept will be aimed at you as a woman. The male staff will, I'm afraid, have to be gorgeous. Either Rob Lowe or Mel Gibson, a whole range of ages. The women more classic, like the elevator pictures. The whole of the staff should feel like a familiar ensemble cast that people will come back to see again and again. But classy – this is not a burger joint. Theory, concept, environment and product. On all four levels The Garden works.'

'This sounds like a fantasy,' Gabrielle said in a goading manner.

'Exactly,' Karen responded. 'Which is why it will work. Daniel?'

'Two months?'

Karen nodded.

'Alan. The costings?' Avendon asked.

'They look fine.'

'This heyday, the Fifties and Sixties you pine on about,' Gabrielle said to her. 'What do you know about them? I suspect of the four people in this room you know the least.'

'It's not just about that, which is why I can make it work. Look at the profiling we've done on our customer base. They don't remember it either, what Hamiltons was like. They don't want to remember, they just want to buy an idea of it. That's what I can sell to them. We can't sell the real thing. It's gone.' Karen breathed deeply at the end of her speech.

'Daniel, remember?' his half-sister said to him. 'They were such times.'

Gabrielle's eyes glazed and she looked as though she were time-travelling. Karen gave Avendon a frustrated look but he took no notice of her. Karen feared he might be about to jump on the same bus as Gabrielle and disappear off down memory lane. Alan seemed faintly embarrassed by Gabrielle's antics.

'Daniel,' Karen said firmly. 'What do you think?'

'Yes. I like it. Very much.'

'Thank you.'

'But—' he paused.

'But?' Karen said.

'I think Gabrielle has a point. I like this retrospective angle. I'm not saying make it a museum, but the original glamour of Hamiltons was something spectacular. Work with Gabrielle on that aspect.'

Karen looked at Gabrielle, who was staring off and looked as though she was about to stand and waltz with a non-existent partner. Karen wished she could smell Gabrielle's breath. She was hoping she was just drunk rather than senile.

'I'd love to help, really I would,' Gabrielle purred, suddenly switching from the wicked witch to Dorothy in the blink of an eye.

'Settled,' said Avendon. 'Good.'

Uncertain whether to feel victorious or defeated, Karen gathered her papers. Gabrielle stood and so did Alan.

'Let's arrange to meet,' Gabrielle said, sweeping out.

Karen stood.

'Wait behind a moment, Karen,' Avendon said, nodding to Alan to leave.

When the door was closed and they were alone, the silence touched all the surfaces in the room. Karen did not know what to say. She was not quite de-railed, more re-routed, but it would still be difficult for her to work with Gabrielle. Eventually, Avendon broke the silence.

'I'm sorry that this has to be so hard for you. Really I am.'

'What do you mean?' she asked.

'Gabrielle has me in a delicate spot. My father saw to it that she remained a very token gesture in the great scheme of the Hamiltons world. By the time he was gone, Gabrielle hated all of us and there was no way to make that better. She can cause a lot of trouble if she wishes.'

'Will she? Why should she?'

'She's had a lawyer look over the structure of her deal with regard to the shop. She has a fifteen per cent stake, but her voting rights were limited and this lawyer thinks a certain part of the contract that regulates it may be unfair. If they challenge it in court and win, she could suddenly be a lot more than just a fifteen per cent pain in the rear. Alan and I have long been aware that the position was somewhat gentle. If she mobilises now, we may have a problem. Despite everything she feels toward me, her holding has always effectively been an Avendon family holding. If she lets it go, we are diluted.'

'How is her helping me going to stop that?' Karen asked him, already resigned to Gabrielle's involvement and realising that this situation had more nuances to it than she first thought.

'She is right, you know. The heyday. I know she can seem ridiculous.' Avendon was looking out of the window. 'She was here and a part of it, until she left. She looks at you and I think she's jealous. She knows she gave up her chance and now she wants it again.'

'Are you saying I should humour her?'

'Perhaps I'm saying you should humour me.'

'And she has no power of veto? I just use her as an advisory resource, like a consultant?' Karen was asking questions, but also laying down some rules.

'It's not something I would ordinarily ask you to do, but it is an unfortunate collision of circumstances and timing. I will be grateful. It's a favour,' he said to her.

'Can I ask you a favour,' she replied. 'Something I wouldn't ordinarily ask?'

'I'm listening.'

'I have a friend who could use a job.'

Chapter Twelve

KAREN TURNED FROM David and reached behind her, picking the phone from her desk.

'Karen Taylor.'

'Karen, it's Linda. How are you?'

'I'm fine,' Karen said, politely motioning for David to leave.

'Thanks for the letter. I'm glad the pictures went down so well,' Linda said, 'and I'm looking forward to seeing them on display myself. Do I get a bottle of the fragrance?'

'I'll ask David my assistant to send you one. I thought we had already, unless it was just to Maxwell. Guess who's staying with me?'

'Give up,' Linda responded instantly.

'Caroline.'

'Caroline Sayer, from college? Dreary Caroline?'

Karen knew that Linda had little time for Caroline and her antics. At college Karen had maintained a discreet kind of Chinese wall between the two friends. Karen supposed she was closer to Caroline, but that was because Caroline was ultimately easier to get closer to. Linda liked a little distance between herself and people and that had never bothered Karen.

'We should try and get together, the three of us,' Karen said.

'Maybe,' Linda responded with little or no enthusiasm. 'I have something to ask you, Karen.'

'Go ahead.'

'It's sort of a favour, but I think you'll like it.'

'I'm still here,' Karen said.

'It's Maxwell.'

'What about him?'

'You have a fan there, Karen. He's burbled on about you for the last four weeks now.'

Karen felt a flush run through her, the sort where she was excited and apprehensive all at once, like a near hit in a car or a drop down a water slide. She had mentioned the video room in Jake's house to no one, having convinced herself that it was simply someone who looked like Maxwell that she had seen up on the screen. Maxwell was talking about her to Linda? She pulled open her desk drawer and retrieved the dove feather she had found on the roof shortly after the shoot, twirling it in her fingers.

'It must be my maternal side coming out,' Karen said to her.

'Some of the things he's been saying about you haven't been very, well, familial.' Linda chuckled dirtily. 'He'd like to meet with you, for a date.'

'I thought you and Maxwell were, well . . .'

'We do, but we're not glued together. He's an attractive boy and I like to think I can still hold my own. We go our own ways. He asked me to call you. He's been on at me about it all week. You must say yes, Karen, or I'll have to contend with a Maxwell tantrum.'

The doves. The hood. The wings. Karen recalled the shoot on the rooftop, his lissom body and the studied way he carried himself. The prospect was inviting. Very inviting. A gift to herself for getting The Garden through. Like a new dress or a special meal. She would treat herself to Maxwell and perhaps she would make it a treat for him as well.

'Are you sure about this, Linda?'

'Come on, Karen, it won't be the first time we've trodden the same ground. Remember Erik the Viking?'

Karen sniggered.

'When would he like to meet?' Karen asked, visions racing through her mind.

'Tonight?' Linda asked her tentatively.

'Tonight.' Karen looked at her diary, knowing already that she had promised to go to dinner with Alan. She could put him off, but he had seemed so excited about taking her out. She chewed her bottom lip on its right side, ruminating. 'I think I can make tonight. Where would he like to go on this date?'

'Just your house, probably, but you can do something else if you want. Before.'

'Christ, say what you mean, Linda. Why don't I just run over there and do him now?'

'Take him for a walk in Hyde Park. He loves it there, the ducks and all the birds. I'm sure he was a bird in a past life.'

'Can he meet me outside the shop, around five?'

'I'm sure he can. I'll call you if not,' said Linda.

'You've got my mobile number, it's on my card.'

'And Karen?'

'Yes?'

'I want to hear all about it.'

'I thought you'd hear that from him.'

'Oh I will,' Linda said, 'but I'd like your opinion as well. Another perspective.'

'I see.' Karen smirked, remembering the way they had compared scores over Erik the Viking at college.

'He likes someone else to take the lead. Don't be shy with him. I haven't found anything he won't do yet.'

'That's a scary thought, Linda,' Karen said.

'Call me tomorrow, okay?'

'Promise.'

Karen replaced the receiver. She picked it straight back up and dialled three digits.

'Alan Saxton.'

'Hi,' she said, breezily.

'Hello,' he said, uncertainty already in his voice. Karen knew he could tell she was about to let him down.

'I've got a problem on tonight,' she said.

'Oh?'

'My friend Caroline, the one I told you about. She wants me to go and help move the last of her stuff tonight. Her boyfriend is back and she wants to get it over here, but doesn't want to face him alone. He's such a pig. Can we reschedule?' Karen always went on too long when she was lying and she wondered when Alan would realise it.

'Of course,' he said, sounding as though he were trying to put a brave face on it.

'Tomorrow?'

'That would be awkward for me. Friday would be good. I could get us theatre tickets, bring the car in,' he said.

'That sounds wonderful. We'll make a night of it. I'm sorry about tonight, Alan. Definitely Friday.'

'You have to help your friends,' he said to her and she cringed, wishing he hadn't said it.

'Thanks for being so understanding. I'll pop round and see you later. Bye.'

Karen sat and stared at the phone. She looked at her watch. It was one-fifteen. She called her flat and spoke to Caroline, telling her she had changed her plans and wouldn't be at Alan's but would be having different company later on at the flat. She also told Caroline to let the machine pick up any calls if she was there when the phone rang. Karen wondered why she made her life so complicated but thought of Maxwell and then it seemed worth it.

Her mind reeling with the expectation of her evening, tempered by some feelings of culpability at putting Alan off, she felt the need to escape her office and Hamiltons so she could both prepare herself for the evening and rid herself of the complications. There was one place she could do both.

'I'm going to the gym,' she said, passing David on her way out. 'I'll probably be back around three-thirty. Leave messages on my mobile or page me if you need to.'

She changed quickly and in a practised fashion. Karen was something of a gym veteran and had been working out since before she was at college. It had paid dividends and she was happy with the shape she had moulded herself into. The gym was through a small doorway just off Knightsbridge and the sort of place where women made up *before* they went to work out. Karen scrutinised herself in the mirror, glad and proud that her skin tone, eye colour and bone structure made make-up an optional extra for her. She wore a tight blue Lycra body suit that supported her breasts and a half-cut jersey grey T-shirt over the top. She carried her New Balance workout shoes by her side and made her way to the stretch area.

At one-forty, the lunchtime crush was starting to ease. Karen preferred to frequent the club at off-peak times, using it purely for the purposes of exercise and never involving herself in the social aspects. Hamiltons paid for her membership and she used it to its fullest, always finding time to exercise at least three times a week. There were only ten or so people in the gym, mostly women, and all the equipment Karen preferred to use was more or less free.

She sat on the mat and looked at herself in the mirror, pulling her feet together and towards her crotch as she dipped her head and felt the stretch in her hips. She leaned deeper into it and then released. She pulled her right foot under her left thigh and leaned forward to elongate her hamstrings, enjoying the relaxing feeling that spread through her leg. Gradually, like a whole flower bed blossoming, she worked through her body, stretching it and letting the elasticity of it take over as she came to a standing position and ended finally by stretching her neck muscles. When she had finished, her muscles were glowing warm and she laced her shoes up.

With the Stairmaster set to a mid level and for a

short time, she did a slow and casual warm up on the machine, her mind already becoming a blank, the images of MTV permeating it and taking hold. The effort required started to increase and she felt her blood begin to flow and her heart speed up, her breathing deeper and much more directed to the simple task of inhaling and expelling air from her lungs. Sweat started to break on her brow and Karen was stepping fast and hard to keep pace with the machine, the red digital readout taunting her with the exertions still to come. She pushed a few buttons to check her effort levels and then looked at the heart monitor attached to her wrist. Karen loved the technology of workouts and on her other wrist was a watch with pre-set times programmed in order to maximise her time and energy in the gym.

Via the Cybex cycle, Karen made her way towards the weights, a mixture of Nautilus machines and free weights. Her current programme had been designed for her by a fearsome South American woman called Dominique and she had used her as a personal trainer for the first two months while she became absolutely familiar with her routine. Karen had been emphatic with Dominique about wanting to cut her physique to a fine and pleasing line and not to stack it up with muscle. She told Dominique that as soon as her body started to look like Madonna's, she wanted to slow it down. That had seemed like an acceptable and amusing goal to Dominique, who looked like she could kill with her bare hands.

Karen worked her major muscle groups on several Nautilus machines and used the free weights for some more specific areas on her arms and back, her breathing steady and regulated and her form and balance in handling the weights perfect. Karen knew that it was too easy to come along to a gym and throw a weight around. Any fool could do that. For her, the workout was more about mind than body. It was an intellectual process where she brought her body into harmony with something external to it and then controlled it. It was only her mind that enabled her to do it. Her demeanour and her attitude. By the end of her session with the weights, she was on another plane completely, glad of the timer on her wrist beeping her out of her reverie. Finally she returned to the mats and did her previous stretching routine but in a much deeper and longer way, her body tired but relaxed, the correct balance between taut and slack.

After a quick shower, Karen sat in the sauna, her thoughts returning to her, but now she had the benefit of seeing them from a different perspective. She poured more water on to the coals and let her body drink steam through its pores, the sensual feel of clean and pure sweat covering her body like a mist. The Garden seemed so clear and so easy to her. Even Gabrielle could be fitted into her plans with little or no disruption and that would do her no damage with Avendon. It had already helped her get Caroline a job, which she hoped would not backfire on her. Tomorrow she would see Alan and talk to him about The Garden, about Gabrielle and about the two of them. She also knew that she had to make some time for Richard in the midst of it all and the thought of his lithe body made her decide that it should be sooner, not later. Slowly, most of her thoughts turned to Maxwell. Something about it seemed so right. She had not realised she had sparked in him something similar to what he had started in her, but obviously she had. A walk in the park, she thought to herself.

Karen spent twenty minutes in the sauna before taking a plunge and a final long and revitalising shower. By the time she was dressed, she felt an incredible calm and serenity. It was four o'clock, somewhat later than she had intended, but then she was a free agent. No one would be looking for her. She went to the bar and ordered a cranberry juice, calling in on her mobile service to David. Nothing major was occurring. She decided to wait in the bar and then wander along to Hamiltons to meet Maxwell at five. She would stow her gym bag in her locker at the club and leave her kit for the laundry service. For forty minutes, she sat and leafed through several papers for work, a couple of magazines and watched the occasional video on MTV. At four forty-five she left, ready for Maxwell.

At first glance, she did not realise it was him. From a distance she saw an unkempt-looking youth in a cobalt blue suit, hair everywhere, and for a moment Karen thought he would ask her for money. By the time she had neared and he was saying hello to her, she realised it was Maxwell. The sandy red hair, the cartoon caricature-like angles of his face and the scar over the right eye all added up to Maxwell. She gripped his hand tightly, holding his thin fingers and feeling the soft cushion of his palm.

'Hello, Karen,' he said, an impish grin spreading a wave of charm which she let ebb pleasantly over her.

'Hi,' she said. 'Do you prefer Maxwell or Max or Maxy?'

He smiled at her. 'Max is nicest. Maxwell was my dad's name and it makes me feel old. My publicity lady doesn't like me to be called Max.'

The solid blue suit was single-breasted and under it he wore a lighter, sky-blue Fred Perry shirt with a red trim, the three buttons all undone to reveal a glimpse of collarbone. His shoes looked as though they had been bought in a charity shop – clumpy black brogues held together by thick laces – and the trousers of the suit were just too long, resting on them as he stood there in Hamiltons' doorway. Despite his scruffy appearance, there was nothing shabby about him. Under the slipshod façade, he was well scrubbed and groomed, the blaze of hair carefully washed and styled and the sweet smell of a recent shower and cologne rising from him. He looked at her, his head held down at an angle as though about to be photographed, and she felt ready to grab him there and then. Why wait, she thought? You are only here to have sex with him, nothing more or less.

'Linda said we should go for a walk in the park,' Maxwell was saying to her, rousing her from her pleasant thoughts.

It would be nice to wait, she thought. To prolong it and tease herself with him.

'That would be nice.'

They were halfway down Sloane Street en route to Knightsbridge, walking side by side and chatting about nothing in particular, when she felt his hand very gently and tentatively slide itself into hers and squeeze.

'Is that all right?' he asked her, looking in front of him, like a marching soldier.

She did not reply but simply exerted some pressure on his hand and continued to look straight ahead. People looked at them but Karen was not sure why. Some may have recognised him or have been troubled because they were sure they knew him from somewhere but couldn't remember where. He exuded a sense of celebrity and presence, his shambolic image a poor disguise for it.

'How did you end up being a model?' she asked him.

'My dad was a film producer and my mum was an actress. Not a very famous one, but she was in a few films. At first, she didn't want me to act or be involved in films or anything. Then she would change her mind and I'd be off doing auditions and things and then she'd change her mind back. One of her friends said to her that they needed someone to model for jeans and that I would be good. It took off from there.'

'What do your parents think about it now?'

He scrunched up his lips and his small slits of eyes, which gave him his asexuality, narrowed impossibly tighter as he considered a reply. Karen traced her thumb over the palm of his hand as it swung gently by their sides.

'My dad died when I was a boy, so I don't know what

he thinks. My mum likes it, I think. My agent is the daughter of an old friend of hers, so she knows I'm looked after and I can do most things I want. She says it's like the next generation of people coming along. Me and the children of all her friends.'

'Do you enjoy it, being photographed?'

'Most of the time. Sometimes I see the pictures, on billboards or in magazines, and it's not me. It's like I'm an actor anyway, even though my mum didn't want me to be. I'm Max down here but up there I'm Maxwell. I enjoy being both.'

Karen listened to him intently, surprised at how level-headed he seemed, clearly having given some thought to the process of his fame. They entered the park and strolled towards the lake, he taking her case from her, having insisted he carry it. She was touched enough by the genuine nature of the gesture to accept. Karen studied his profile, seeing the perfectly constructed features from a different angle – the snub of his nose and the pout of his lips and the way his brow furrowed into a moody shape. Through the images she had seen of him, those features had been moulded and trained, giving off different messages at different times. Seeing him in the flesh, watching him as he spoke, she was witnessing him in full flow, the expressiveness of his face running in time with his words, often saying more than the words themselves.

They came to rest on a bench by the lake, people hurrying around them as they made their various ways home. In the midst of the hubbub, Karen felt relaxed, still glowing from her session at the gym, enjoying Maxwell and anticipating the prospect of an interesting evening. He sat sideways on the bench so he could face her and stared at her intently, deeply interested in her.

'Linda says you're really good at your job,' he said to her.

'I suspect you would say that. And her too,' Karen laughed.

He laughed as well. 'Honestly, she did,' he said persuasively, his eyes scanning the bench and quickly running over her before averting their gaze.

'I am good at what I do. They give me enough room to be, that's the important thing.'

'You've known her since college?' Maxwell asked.

'Linda? She was one of my best friends there. We had some good times.'

'I like Linda,' Maxwell said. 'She's a challenge sometimes.'

'You don't have to tell me that. I've had some horrible rows with her because she's so wilful.' She looked at him as she spoke, her mouth saying one thing, her mind in a million other places, recalling the photo shoot, the video room at Jake's, Maxwell and Max himself.

'I bet you're just as stubborn as her,' he said to her.

'I don't know. I hate the way women are always called stubborn or bitchy if they have some, any, kind of power.'

'Can I kiss you?' he asked her nervously.

'Do you want to?'

'I wouldn't ask unless I did.'

She leaned towards him, pushing her face and, by extension, her lips, forward. He was there to meet them and their mouths were joined, the air between them suddenly becoming common, and she tightly locked herself in a gesture of tenderness with someone she barely knew. Karen pouted and twisted her lips, her hand coming up to cradle the back of his head as he craned further forward to get at her. Karen leaned further sidewards and brought her other hand into his jacket and ran it along his side, the roughness of the Fred Perry shirt against her skin. Her hand wandered down and then up the shirt, feeling his hip where it touched the waistband of his trousers. She was ready to take him home.

They wandered back, Karen keeping her desire under control and Maxwell looking at pigeons and ducks, even talking to them occasionally. The birdboy of Alcatraz, Karen thought to herself. Where they had said much on the way there, the walk back was punctuated by only the occasional comment, the silence one of anticipation more than nerves. When they were in the lift on the way up to her apartment, he spoke in a low tone.

'I want you to do me,' he said, pushing into her with his groin as though his libido had suddenly gone up a gear.

'What do you want me to do?' she asked.

'Anything you want. Everything you want. Did Linda tell you I'll try anything?'

When he moved against her again, coyly coaxing her with his body, she felt the hardness in his groin.

'What does Linda do with you?' she asked, intrigued and excited at the thought of them together.

'All sorts.' He was whispering dirtily in her ear. 'She ties me up, hits me, sticks things in me. I love it. Feel.'

He grabbed her hand and pushed it into his crotch. She gripped his cock through the blue material and it grew even in the brief seconds that she held it. He looked at her the whole time she was on him. The lift bumped to a halt and she released him, composing herself before the door opened.

'Where's the bedroom?' he asked her as she put the key in her front door.

'Third on the left. You're keen,' she said, opening the door.

'I loved you in New York, by the way,' he said as he ran past her, laughing and heading for the bedroom door.

'Max!' she shouted after him, pausing to close the door.

When she reached the bedroom, he had already kicked off the beaten-up black brogues and removed his socks. He looked up at her, his head dropped in the familiar posing manner, an expectant and dirty look on his face as though he had suddenly gone from Jekyll to Hyde.

'Do you want me dressed or undressed?' he asked her.

'I want to know what you mean about New York,' she said to him, a confused anger simmering in her.

'At Jake's house,' he said, casually sitting down on her bed and staring up at her.

'You know Jake?'

'Friend of the family. Of my mother's, actually.'

'Does your mother know what you do for Jake?'

He laughed at her. 'You sound more like my mother than she does. Does yours know what *you* do there?'

'When did you see me there?'

'When you were in the monitor room. I watched you on a video tape where you were watching me on a video. And I saw the video of you and Chris Nichol. Very nice.'

'You weren't actually there at the time?' Karen asked, feeling spooked retrospectively.

'No, don't be silly. I saw it afterwards.'

'I talked to Jake about you, just to test the water. He didn't say he knew you,' Karen challenged.

'We keep our friendship very private. Do you want me dressed or undressed?'

Karen was angry and excited, the mix a potent one. She would have words with Jake later, but right at that moment, Maxwell was the nearest thing to hand and she was prepared to take it out on him.

'Get undressed,' she said snappily, a small satisfied smile on her face as he quickly complied.

She stared at his nude form, scrutinising in the flesh and up close what she had seen in person, on paper and in film in the previous weeks. The agile and hairless figure was appetising to behold. She held him in her silent scrutiny, waiting until he would start to feel nervous in her presence. Her examination was cool, long and unforgiving, revealing nothing to him about her thoughts. As he shifted from foot to foot, his hand touching his stiff cock, she knew she had reached the uncomfortable stage for him. So she continued to appraise him, wondering how it felt for him, someone so used to being looked at by millions of people, to stand and be looked at by only one. He gave a loud and tight swallow. Karen had locked him to the spot with the power of her gaze and she felt his timidity as surely as if she could have reached out and touched it. She decided it was time to release him from it.

'Lie face down on the bed,' she said to him.

While he did so, Karen slipped out of her own clothes, all the time observing the naked form on her bed, the curve of his rear barely perceptible, the shoulder blades bony and the arms thin extensions from the slight torso. She went to her case and retrieved the feather.

Kneeling next him on the bed, Karen traced the feather down from between his shoulders into the small of his back and airily over his buttocks, sweeping a circle around his rear before lighting the feather along the rift where his cheeks met. He quivered and shuddered under the touch, the feather able to cause movements far out of proportion to its exquisite graze. Between her legs, Karen felt a moistness and a longing, her earlier anger forgotten and replaced by the urge she had for him.

Down the backs of his legs and over the soles of his feet she whisked the feather, making him giggle and fidget on the mattress, his whole torso wiggling at her teasing touch. She played it against the nape of his neck, pushing it under his hair and watching it emerge from beneath the thatch. He turned his head to one side and she stroked his cheek with it, moving her body closer to his, the feeling of skin on skin. She tickled under his arms and he cried out, telling her it was not fair. She then flicked it where she knew he wanted it most.

Karen knelt between his open legs and brushed the underside of his balls with the feather. He let out a long and low groan that reverberated around the room and through the mattress. Opening his legs further he raised himself up, reaching to push his balls further down under himself so they were on display for Karen. She skimmed the surface of his ball sac, watching the wrinkled skin move under her caress, occasionally running the feather up the crack of his taut bottom.

'Turn over, Max,' she said.

Instantly he was on his back, his hand grabbing at his cock.

'Leave that alone until I tell you,' she said and it was instantly let go, slapping against the bottom of his stomach with a satisfying crack. She would get to his cock eventually, but it was her turn now.

Straddling his chest first, Karen wriggled her way up until she was over his face, her knees planted either side of his head. Her bottom touched his chest lightly and as she reared up, her pussy was suspended several inches from his pretty face, his hands stuck close to his sides. The view of his face from her position consisted mostly of the top half, his nose just visible and his green eyes glassy. She toyed at herself with the feather, stroking it lightly against her pussy-lips. Behind them, she felt herself swell and fill with juices that sprang from the very centre of herself, a tangible expression of the seething hunger that was gripping her like a vice. The feather was agonising as it whistled against her lips, rustling her dark pubic hair as she felt the gush of her juices held back by her like a dam.

When she was ready to burst, she discarded the feather, reached down and gently opened her lips with two fingers. A small droplet, like the first sign of rain, escaped her and tumbled onto Maxwell's high cheekbone, his eyes widening from their slit-like shape as it did so. Karen moved herself back so that she was more directly over his mouth.

'Keep your mouth closed until I tell you to open it,' she ordered him. He nodded.

She opened herself wider, and put her hand on her clitoris, feeling the gentle rush of breath through Max's nose. She pressed into herself, her fingers indenting the soft area around the peak of her desire, signals transmitting through her whole body as a light shiver ran up her back. She looked down at his face, wet with her and she spoke.

'Open your mouth.'

He licked around his lips, his tongue long and pointed, taking her juices and tasting them. She dipped lower, bringing her pussy perilously close to the lashing tongue, playfully pulling away as it neared her, allowing it to catch her once or twice. His arms were still pressed against his side, held in check by Karen's legs. She retrieved the feather and deftly spun around, her rear resting on his chest. As she did so, Maxwell freed his arms and she soon felt his hands smoothing over her cheeks.

Karen looked at his cock. Long, quite thin, very stiff and a large wide head. His pubic hair was the same light sandy colour as that on his head. Raising her backside and leaning forward, she began to work at his cock with the feather, listening to his cries as she did so. She was determined to prolong the agony for as long as she could, wondering if she could eventually bring him to orgasm with the feather. It seemed a likely a prospect, judging by the jerking movements his member was making. The skin that sheathed the shaft seemed barely able to keep it in check as it burst forth from him, seeming out of scale to his frame.

There was a flurry of movement from Max and then Karen felt the rough wetness of a tongue skimming the sensitive area of skin that marked the pathway between her pussy and her anus. His hands were opening her cheeks and Karen could feel him flecking away at her, the tongue leaving small spots of wetness as evidence of its presence. His tongue made a journey further upward and she gasped as it moistened her anus, the wrinkled pucker feeling suddenly more elastic from his licking. Maxwell's cock momentarily forgotten, Karen placed her hands on his stomach, just under his ribs, and raised herself more upright, allowing him to burrow his tongue lightly into her anus. As he did so, she gripped him, feeling his ribs under her palms. For several long moments she allowed him to probe her, to enter his long pointed tongue into her behind.

From far inside of her a guttural cry escaped, a desperate whimper of passion, and she was off his tongue, rushing down his body to get at his cock. With her back still to him, she straddled him and roughly shoved his cock inside her, he crying out from the painfully upright angle at which she held him and she from the feel of such a rough and delightfully quick penetration. The angle of their bodies made only a very short penetrative depth possible, but it was sharp and ruthless enough for Karen and concentrated much of the sensation on her clitoris. She supported herself on one hand and writhed her body quickly, shifting Max's cock in and out of her pussy with a vengeance.

Moistening a finger with her own juices, Karen reached under Max's legs and down between the cleft of his rear, and he moved his legs helpfully. He whimpered contentedly as she fingered him, massaging him in time with her lunges on to his body. His anus was tight and her finger was held tightly by it.

He called out to her, telling her he was about to come. Karen speeded her movements up, both her finger and her whole body, pushing herself to get where she had been aiming since they had met that first afternoon on the roof. Unable to see him, only to feel his cock in her and her finger in him, she closed her eyes and let the images of him from the previous weeks engulf her. It was not the doves nor the falcon nor the leather hood which finally pushed her into flight. It was what Linda had described as the Forlorn Angel picture where he had been sitting wearing small wings held to his body by leather straps and had sadly

133

surveyed the London skyline. He had looked so vulnerable, ready to leap off and take flight at any moment. Karen formulated the image in her mind and forced it to stay there as long as possible before her orgasm would rip it from her mind and spread it all over her body, translating images into feelings.

With broken and desperate cries, she relinquished him to her whole body, the forlorn angel now shaking throughout her, her pussy undulating from the deep intensity of the orgasm. Around her finger, Max's anus tightened and he grunted. Karen slowed the movements of her pussy on his cock but kept the same relentless rhythm inside him, making him cry out and beg her to stop. She did not. All the way through his orgasm, as he throbbed into her and contracted around her digit, she continued to finger at him, trying to imagine the agony and the pleasure she was giving him as he ejaculated long and hard into her pussy.

When they were done, she released him. She turned and lay back on the bed, out of breath and covered in a sheen of sweat. Maxwell put an arm over her and nuzzled himself under her arm, his head resting on her shoulder and his still-quivering cock touching her side. She pulled him to her and he squeezed her. As she rested her face into his sandy hair, the cologne still sweet to her nostrils, she stroked the skin on his shoulders and kissed at his forehead. He was wordless and seemed anxious to get close to her and be intimate, as though it was all he had left to give.

In the warmth and the closeness of their bodies, her arms wrapped around him like wings, they slept.

Chapter Thirteen

HAVING NEGOTIATED THE central London traffic late on a Friday night, Karen and Alan were on the west side of London heading out to his other house in Berkshire.

'I've had such a nice evening,' he said to her, concentrating on the road and steering the large car round a bend with ease.

'Me too. Thank you.'

As he had promised, Alan had booked theatre tickets and they had been to a play at the National Theatre and then on to dinner. Just the two of them, as always. Karen had gone home after work and changed into a dramatic Claude Montana opera coat with a fine wool crew neck and light silk skirt underneath. The cloth moved in a theatrical fashion and she liked the feel of it around her. At the end of a hectic Friday spent on the phone and in meetings, all connected with The Garden, she was tired enough to have just dropped straight into bed when she got home, but was glad she had decided to see Alan. She felt she had neglected him in general over the past several weeks and she still felt guilty for putting him off two days earlier, when she had seen Maxwell. He had been so helpful with The Garden and for that reason alone she did not want to do anything that might hurt him.

The play had engaged her and the dinner had

relaxed her. They shared easy and familiar conversation, laughing and giggling, and Karen was conscious of the ways in which they were becoming comfortable with each other. Still, Alan's suggestion that they travel to the house in Berkshire had caught her off-guard. Karen knew he had a house there, but did not expect to be invited to it, such an invitation seeming to signal a progression to a further stage in their friendship. Since Karen was not entirely sure she wanted to enter such a stage, she had hesitated, but it was a Friday and she was curious to see it.

'Which house did you have first? The one out here or the one in Fulham?' she asked him, not mentioning his recently ex-wife.

'The one out here. Fulham came quite a bit later, once we'd settled on not having any family.'

Karen listened to his voice in the dim light of the car, wondering if he was happy to talk to her about it. 'Why did you settle on the idea of no family? Couldn't you?'

'We could have, but didn't. We lived in a lot of places around London to be near Hamiltons and the Inns of Court, but the house out here was a stable weekend retreat. It was fun because we could always pick odd or off-the-wall kinds of places to live in London, like we were still students.'

'Do you wish you had children?'

He hesitated, staring ahead at the road, not speaking. She was about to ask the question again.

'I do wish that, yes.'

'You met Margaret at Cambridge, didn't you?'

'Yes. She was all those sorts of things people mention when they go glassy-eyed and talk in clichés. Funny, clever, attractive, sharp and forthright. She was all of those, much more than I could have been.'

'And still is?'

'Probably. Sorry, I know I shouldn't talk about her in the past tense, as though she were dead. If she were dead, I wouldn't be able to use the present tense.' He glanced over at her and smiled at the mock evil in his tone.

'You don't really wish that, do you?'

'Only sometimes, and never as bad as I used to.'

'Was it hard to get divorced after all that time?'

'Yes. Very hard. Never divorce a lawyer,' he laughed with a trace of bitter-sweet. 'That's not fair actually. I did well. Both houses, but then she hated both of them.'

'You're lucky to have two houses,' Karen said to him.

'Hamiltons has been good to me. Anyway, your flat sounds nice. Convenient. I look forward to seeing it sometime.'

'Hint taken,' she said.

They had left the motorway and were on a small lane, narrow, unlit and bending, the beams of the headlights illuminating the road far ahead, insects lit by the beacons of light.

'Here we are,' Alan said, turning into a driveway, the solid sound of the road giving way to the crunch of gravel.

A security light lit the front of the house as they approached it. Long and low with a double front, a garden that seemed to be well-kept even in the darkness, the house was very countrified, particularly to Karen's urban gaze. As she stepped from the car, gown flowing, her breath was visible in the chill midnight air.

Inside, it was a rural version of Alan. All the city things that she associated with his house in Fulham, the art nouveau antiques and the slightly jazzy decoration, were toned and refined to an air of sedate and expensive taste. Karen could tell it was his house as soon as she entered it. He gave her a quick tour, showing her around upstairs first and then the downstairs, which had been extended off either end of the house to yield a large kitchen and a small studio.

'Margaret liked, sorry, likes, to paint. We built this

137

eight, no, nine years ago. She used to come out here and paint.'

The air in the studio smelled of white spirit and all the surfaces were perfectly clean, no trace of paint anywhere. Karen wondered if Alan had scrubbed it down after she had left.

'Do you have any pictures of her?' Karen asked him.

'Somewhere. You don't really want to see them, do you?'

'Only if you don't mind. I'm curious to see her, that's all. If it's too awkward for you . . .'

'Of course not,' he said to her. 'Let's go to the drawing-room and I'll fix us a nightcap and dig out an album or two.'

Sipping brandy from a huge glass, Karen sat on a sofa in the drawing-room – a mixture of greens and whites and dark oak furniture. She had casually discarded the opera coat and was enjoying the new freedom of movement afforded by its absence, while Alan sat next to her and flicked through an old book of photographs. Margaret was very striking, although she did not say so to Alan. Her eyes were piercing, black almost, and she glared at the camera in almost every photograph as though extremely angry with the photographer.

'She's not what I expected,' Karen managed finally.

'She had all but stopped attending any of the Hamiltons functions by the time you arrived, otherwise you would have got to meet her.'

'You don't think she'll be a customer at The Garden, then?'

'Not Margaret, I'm afraid. A few years ago, possibly, but not now.'

'Is she involved with anyone else at the moment?' Karen asked.

'Another lawyer,' was his short and simple reply.

'At the same firm?'

'No, she wouldn't do that. Not like us,' he answered.

'Does she know we're seeing each other?'

'Karen, I don't think anyone knows we're seeing each other, it's been such a state secret.'

'That's the best way though Alan, really.

'Who's that?' she asked, pointing to a colour snap of a boy, a typical first-day-of-school photograph. A brave smile on a presumably cold September morning.

'Oh, that,' Alan said, his mind appearing to fumble. 'His name is John. A nephew of Margaret's. Good-looking boy.'

Karen looked at the boy and could see that he would have grown up to be quite cute.

'When was this taken?' she laughed. 'He might be worth meeting.'

'Oh, I don't think so,' he said quietly, and Karen thought he seemed upset by her comment, jealous almost.

'I was only teasing, darling, really,' she said, never having called him darling before.

She let her hand drop on to his arm and he closed the book.

'I know you were. How are you getting on with Gabrielle?' he asked.

'It's not as bad as I thought it would be. She's more like noise in the background, interference. She doesn't seem to have any agenda that relates to me, so it's not so hard.'

'Her agenda,' he said, placing emphasis on the word agenda and showing it as one he would not normally use, 'is very much related to Daniel.'

'There must be such a bad history between them.'

'Yes, but it's none of their doing. It all happened because of their parents and they were caught up in it, Gabrielle especially. Daniel was more protected. I think his father saw to that.'

'What was Lawrence Avendon like?'

'He was a bastard. Not even a fair bastard, just a bastard. I may have joked about wanting to kill Margaret, but when Lawrence died, Daniel felt such a mixture of emotions. I don't think he ever recovered.'

The conversation had come to a natural conclusion. In the silence that ensued between them, Karen listened to the sound of the room and the whole house around her. A clock ticked in the background, metronomic and precise, and she felt the presence of the past, the history of Alan and of Hamiltons. It was strange to be involved in something that had so much of a past, the true story of which she was certain she did not know. Deep down, she wondered if part of her logic for getting involved with Alan in the first place was to try and connect to some of the legend and myth of Hamiltons, to make her feel a part of it. That may have been true, she thought, but at that moment she wanted nothing more than to connect with Alan in a very basic and physical way, regardless of the reasons or the implications.

Karen felt a tingle of excitement as her desire for Alan slowly worked its way through her, obliterating all her other feelings, and she let the sensation wash away at her, smothering any doubts she had about their relationship. Reaching out across the small distance between them, she rested her hand on his knee, feeling the power of even such a simple connection. Still there were no words, only the sense of touch, her hand on the material of his trousers. Carefully, Alan set the photograph album to rest on the floor along with the other one and when he had done so, he placed his hand over hers. Karen could sense that he was thinking about speaking and she could almost hear his thoughts, which were the same as her own. 'This won't work. We're too different. Our ages. Our positions at Hamiltons.' Karen had other, supplementary thoughts of her own about Richard and about The Garden and she hoped that Alan was not aware of those. But, despite all the unspoken words between them, the thoughts and reservations, the power of feeling was too strong. Karen moved her hand higher, resting it on his thigh, taking his hand with hers.

Alan led her by the hand up into a bedroom that was very floral in a Laura Ashley way. The bed was large, king-sized, with a heavy brass bedstead. For a long silent moment they faced each other at one side of the bed, the atmosphere heavy with the expectation of sex. Alan lifted her crew-neck over her head and as it was removed she shook her head a fraction, letting her short hair swing as freely as it could. Alan's face was concentrating closely on his task as he removed her bra, unzipped her skirt and then unclipped her stockings. Her knickers and suspender belt followed immediately, as though Alan was not interested in the titillation of her underwear, wanting only her. He had not rushed in his undressing of her, but nor had he lingered, his need for her seeming to have found a speed which was comfortable for them both. With a similar pace, he removed his own clothes while Karen looked on.

As she stood, he reached out and rubbed at her hip bones, his thumbs gently pressuring the trim flesh that led towards her pubic hair. His hands spread themselves and roved around her hips and made a cupping shape on her behind, squeezing it gently before his strong fingers delicately splayed and ran up her sides, the lightness of the touch tickling like a feather. Karen breathed heavily as he fondled her breasts, pressing at the soft flesh and pulling on her nipples, holding each between a finger and thumb. With each pinch, she closed her eyes and felt gravity change around her and her head become light. With his hands back on her hips, he kissed her and carefully steered her on to the bed.

Where he had used his hands when she stood, now, as she lay on the bed, he replaced them with the brush of his lips, nibbling at her hips where they pointed through the skin and nuzzling at the border of her pubic hair. His mouth made her nipples wet, causing them to stand out still further, the sensitive nerve-endings of her lust on display for him. He bit carefully at them and rolled them about in his teeth, alternating from one breast to the other, never lingering too long on either. He kissed her throat and the skin under her jaw and then the jaw-line itself, finishing up back on her mouth. Karen held his head and stroked his hair.

Alan produced a small bottle of massage oil and unhurriedly removed its top. The aroma of spicy orange pervaded the atmosphere around the bed. Karen lay, a warm and slack feeling all over her. He began with her shins and the tops of her feet, spreading a fine film of oil over them and moving his hands fluidly back and forth. His hand felt large as it moved around over her inner thighs, grazing closely over the top of her pussy and then pulling back, retracting itself to give her tightly muscled leg a squeeze. Karen enjoyed the pressure he exerted on her stomach as he covered it in a veneer of oil, his hands making a sound just discernible as they moved about her. On her breasts, he used more than elsewhere and they were soon slippery in his hands, occasionally escaping his attempts to squeeze them.

After he had oiled her arms, he gently turned her over and finished off the bottom of her feet and the backs of her legs. Karen felt the oil pouring on to her behind and then Alan's hands kneaded her buttocks, squeezing and pushing them together, the side of his hand occasionally in the cleft. Finally, he concentrated long and hard on her back and shoulders and she felt the knots of the day undo themselves as he pushed his fingers expertly into her flesh. Karen wondered if he had ever been trained to massage, since his touch was so firm and relaxing. When he was done, she turned on to her back and looked at him as he gazed silently down at her.

Needing no oil, Alan worked his hand at Karen's pussy. As he leaned over her, one hand supporting himself, his cock hung from him in a swollen erection. He toyed with her as though deliberately holding back as long as possible both on her and himself. Karen opened her outspread legs an inch or two further and Alan continued to push his middle finger in and out of her, stopping only to apply pressure to the area around her clitoris. He had worked over her whole body, preparing her, and had now come to rest on this single area. His pace was steady and continuous and Karen felt the results of his earlier lengthy preparation approaching as she shifted herself on the bed and closed her eyes.

Karen made barely a sound as she came, communicating her pleasure to him through movement alone. She arched her back off the bed and pulled at her nipples, which were slippery to the touch. Several times in short succession she lifted herself from the bed using her feet and shoulders as pivots. Her head flicked back rhythmically, a deep contraction in her neck forcing it regardless of her will. Dropping back on to the bed she closed her legs, feeling oily foot on oily foot, and gripped Alan's hand, pushing it harder into her. Her vagina swelled around his finger and her movements subsided as she passed the peak of her orgasm. Squeezing his hand and removing it from her, she gripped it and lay on the bed, letting her breathing regulate.

When she opened her eyes, he was kneeling there and gazing at her intensely, his cock still looking painfully hard. The grey eyes feasted on her and his hair hung carelessly over his forehead, the streaks of grey caught by the lamp looking like small forks of lightning. She pulled herself upright using his hand and took the oil bottle from the foot of the bed where it rested against the bedstead. Pouring a large helping into her palm, she transferred it to his cock, beginning at the base near his balls and working up over the tip. The noises her hand made were liquid and she squeezed his shaft, enjoying the way it slipped and slid about as though trying to escape her. The movement of her hand was easy, the lubricant effect of the oil allowing her to trace a path over him, both her hands working on him at the same time, passing each other but never meeting. She clutched him hard and then released him, watching the way the blood pulsed and he swelled, the oil making his cock shine in the soft light of the room. Circling her finger tightly around the base of his cock, she studied it for a moment before she took it back in her whole hand, clenching it tightly, and lying back down on the bed, bringing him over her at the same time.

Alan reached his hand above her head and pulled a pillow from under the bed-cover. Knowing what he wanted to do, Karen raised her behind so he could place it on the bed, but not before he had doubled it over to maximise the height it would give her. Karen felt her body tilted back into the bed and she drew her legs up, which made them feel heavier and as though they were trying to gravitate towards her head. Partially giving in to the sensation, she allowed her knees to fall sideways towards the bed and her feet to hang inwards. As Alan leaned over her, so she felt that the angle of their bodies was perfectly aligned and that she was ready to be penetrated by him.

The penetration was silent and precise. She whimpered as his oiled cock slid between her lips and into her upraised pussy. Holding her legs behind the knees and pulling them back further, she allowed Alan's weighty cock the access it needed. In what seemed a very short space of time, he had entered her and his pubic hair was against her own, their bodies joined at the groin. Karen's shoulders were pushed back into the mattress by the position of her body on the bed with the pillow underneath her.

With a beat and speed that was similar to the way his finger had been earlier, Alan began to move himself in and out of her. Like all of their sex so far that night, he started in a relaxed and unhurried manner. This gradual and careful pace allowed Karen to focus on the very precise nature of their coupling, the way her vagina moulded itself to him and the way his cock stimulated her both inside and out. She pushed her head back and stretched the muscles in her neck and down the whole of her back. Her body was still nicely oiled from the massage and her muscles were warm. Feeling completely at ease, Karen moved her head from side to side on the bed, running her hands through her hair as she did so and making little noises of pleasure.

Inside her Alan's cock felt firmly planted and as it became more engorged, so it expanded Karen around him. He was pulling out as far as he could before making a determined drive back into her and Karen admired his control, sensing he could easily go over the edge, as she had earlier and was now ready to do again. For several seconds, she opened her eyes and rejoined him, watching his hair flick from his exertion and his face change as the tenor of his passion for her grew. Karen reached up and touched his sides, the slight contour of his biceps there, and she moved her hands down a little further and used them to make encouraging movements in time with his own, coaxing him to go faster into her.

When his speed had built up and his face contorted further, Karen closed her eyes and concentrated on herself, leaving the work to Alan. The darkness of her closed eyes seemed to become lighter and she felt herself drift around in her head, as though weightless and roaming free in there, not bounded by specific thoughts but once again guided only by sensation. Alan's increasingly frantic movements pushed her against the mattress, but after a while she became less conscious of the specifics of his movement and what became important was the impression it left on her thoughts. Even the sounds he made became less audible to Karen and all her feelings wove themselves together as she felt her orgasm stir.

It was an amplified version of her earlier peak, when Alan had been using only his finger. This time, however, Karen released all the feelings that had been building in her since they had arrived at the house and let them flow through into a long and loud cry. The thrusting became more erratic and Karen felt warmth flow into her with sharp jets, his cries mingling with her own. Karen's body snapped with whip-like motions as the orgasm brought her to attention and against this rigidity Alan thrashed at her, spilling wildly into her.

While Alan slept, his breathing getting deeper and more rhythmic as the minutes passed, Karen lay staring into the darkness, making out unfamiliar shapes in a strange room.

Earlier, her feelings had led her down the path to sex, ignoring the words that she knew should have passed between them and would possibly have held her back – perhaps held the both of them back. As she drifted into sleep, Karen wondered how long it would be before she could find the words that would lead her down the other path. The path that led away from Alan.

Chapter Fourteen

KAREN LOOKED OVER at Caroline as they went through the doors of Hamiltons. Caroline was tugging at the tweed suit by Isaac Mizrahi, the one Karen had loaned her that morning. Formal and double-breasted, it made the best of her shoulders and tapered in at her hips. Caroline insisted on trying to pull the skirt down until it was almost like a hipster in order to give it more length.

'Stop it,' Karen said to her, slapping her on the arm at the same time.

'Sorry!' Caroline replied. 'I'm nervous.'

'Everything will be fine.'

'I've never got a job without even having to interview before. It's worse than having the interview.'

'Caroline, it's only a temporary job. I told you that.'

'I know, but working for Daniel Avendon. You must have pulled strings.'

Karen smiled and did not reply for a moment, waiting until they were in the store and, as was her practice, riding the escalator.

'Believe me, my strings are being pulled substantially more than his,' she said, frowning as Caroline fingered the hem of the skirt.

Karen herself wore a stone grey outfit by Jil Sander – a short dress with a vest-like top whose round and low neck-line stopped just short of her cleavage. Her nipples showed through the material and the perilously short skirt was redeemed by a marginally longer one of identical colour and material that flowed from underneath it. A loosely constructed top finished off the outfit, which was cool and easy to move in. She wore discreet earrings that were Chanel, a present from a former flame, and she had sprayed herself in Coco, matching fragrance to accessories. As they made their slow ascent, she said hello to several people.

'Does everyone here know you?' Caroline asked her.

'More or less.'

'When do I get to see the two lovers then?'

'Caroline, discretion please. Here we are.' Karen led her through the door marked 'Private' and into the office area on the fifth floor.

Karen introduced Caroline to Avendon's secretary. She had been worried that getting her this assignment would have upset Daniel's full-time PA, but it had not. They went in to meet Daniel, who was in the middle of punching a number into the telephone. When he saw them, he stopped, smiled and placed the receiver down, standing to greet them. Karen forgot occasionally how charming and charismatic Avendon could be, not unlike Alan but with the benefit of several million more pounds. He moved across the floor as though wearing dancing shoes, gliding over French chalk.

'Karen, hello. This is Caroline?' Avendon said, bathing her in his full attention.

'Pleased to meet you. I'm Caroline,' she said extending her hand, the other playing at the skirt. Karen wanted to kick her, but resisted.

'Excellent. Fine,' Avendon said.

'Thank you for giving me the chance to help out,' Caroline was saying.

'I'm sure you won't thank me. This filing project rolls around every six or so months and I won't have Jane do it any more. She's my PA. You met her on the way in, presumably. She can show you what needs doing.'

'Caroline, as I said, Daniel, is a very experienced office worker in a number of contexts. She'll have no problems, I'm sure,' Karen said.

'If she does, I'll just hold you responsible,' Avendon said, holding the silence at the end of his sentence for a second before booming out a laugh. Karen saw the relief spread over Caroline's face as her hands ferreted away at the Isaac Mizrahi and she wondered if this had been such a good idea.

'I'll introduce Caroline to Jane properly,' Karen said, grabbing her up and jockeying her out, 'and then if you have a moment, I'd like to pop back?'

'Certainly.'

'That wasn't so bad, was it?' Karen asked. 'Except for when you nearly ripped the skirt off. I think he thought you were a strip-o-gram I'd hired for a joke.'

'It's too short,' Caroline said.

'Never for Daniel,' she replied. 'Jane, can you show Caroline what she needs to do?'

She left Caroline, imagining how a mother feels when her child starts school, and went back to Daniel's office.

'How are things in The Garden? Rosy?' Avendon asked when she returned.

'Very. I have a meeting with Gabrielle on the floor in about ten minutes,' Karen said.

'I know. She has been here and went down there a half hour ago. She was surprised, I think, at how well advanced things were.'

'We agreed, Daniel, that she would have some consultative input into this. That doesn't mean she gets to design the thing from ground up. It wouldn't have been appropriate to involve her too deeply before now.'

'I agree. I'm not questioning.' He clenched his hands and rolled his thumbs around each other as he spoke. 'Simply reporting. I do appreciate her having this outlet. The launch of the fragrance and The Garden will still be on schedule?'

'Definitely, unless there's a catastrophe of some sort.'

'Wonderful.'

'I wanted to say thank you again for letting Caroline help out. She's had a bad time lately.'

'Glad to. A bit of back-scratching. She seems lively enough – a bit fidgety, perhaps.' Avendon grinned.

'I'll come by and take her out for a long lunch a bit later. See how she's coping. See if she's found anything incriminating in all that filing.'

'My dear, Jane shreds that long before it gets to this stage. And the real scandal?' He tapped his head, 'Is all in here.'

Before going to meet Gabrielle, she conferred with David, he reading items off his clipboard, ticking as he went. He had been helpful in humouring Gabrielle when she was trying to contact Karen over the previous weeks, and she was sure that Gabrielle had taken a liking to him, something she had teased him about. 'I'd be like one of those dancing boys Eartha Kitt has on stage,' he had said to her in horror.

'How was your friend?' he asked.

'As well as can be. I'll take you to lunch with her some time and you can meet her for yourself. She's capable once she gets going, it's just that initial kick.'

David sniffed before beginning his next sentence and Karen braced herself at this signal of a gripe to come. 'Richard Fraser was up here looking for you Friday night, after you'd left. He was rude to me as usual. Could you ask him not to be? Tell him just because he's *fucking* my boss, that doesn't *make* him my boss.'

'David!' she said in surprise. 'Who says I'm fucking him?'

'The list of who doesn't would be shorter,' he trilled.

Karen, even after her considerable time there, was still surprised at how completely impossible it was to keep a lid on anything at Hamiltons. She wondered if Alan knew. He would probably say something to her if she did.

'Do you think Daniel or anyone like that knows?' she asked him, trying to make the question sound general.

'No, I don't think Alan knows,' he said, intoning heavily. 'And don't worry, I think I'm the only one who knows you're fucking Alan.'

She looked at him, wanting to laugh and wanting to slap him at the same time.

'David, sometimes.'

'Any chance of Richard coming our way when you're done with him?' David asked, a fragment of genuine hope in his voice.

'More chance of Alan coming your way, I think. Thanks for letting me know, David. And thanks for keeping it quiet. I need to sort it out,' she told him.

'Choices, choices,' he said to her. 'Bane of my life.'

The area set aside for The Garden was at the back half of the furniture department on the fourth floor. It was certainly the most logical area of the shop in which to house her project both commercially and architecturally. A number of false walls had been taken down, including some offices at the very back, and a huge expanse had opened up in their wake. With the wide open space there, a new false wall was erected, floor to ceiling, completely sealing off the space that would become The Garden. A number of the display sofas from the old department had been retrieved and were off being re-covered for use in The Garden.

Cabinets and display areas had already been planned by a specialist retail agency and a group of shopfitters were currently working on them plus the lighting, which was being done by a contract firm. Following this, what Karen referred to as 'the green people' would arrive. It was a plant and flower hire company that would make The Garden into the lush and verdant paradise Karen imagined it to be.

As she walked through the door that bore the sign

apologising for the inconvenience, it was difficult to imagine the ambience and how it would really be. Still, this was halfway towards the realisation of what had been nothing more than a notion only seven weeks ago. A feeling of satisfaction swept over Karen at the way she would be able to make The Garden real. Several workmen were ambling around, carrying or shifting building materials. When the department was open, the door through which she had just entered would be sealed off to the public, their only access being the lift that ran up the back of the building. Karen made her way over to it, to appreciate how the customer would first see The Garden, and as she neared, she heard the strains of an argument.

'What seems to be the problem?' Karen asked, planting herself between Gabrielle and the foreman.

'This man will not listen,' Gabrielle said petulantly.

Karen turned to Malcolm, the foreman, and looked at him apologetically.

'Malcolm, I'll come speak with you in a moment,' she said in an even and friendly way, using her eyes to indicate whose side she was on.

Disgruntled, he turned and was gone.

'What's the matter, Gabrielle?' she asked.

'I told him that we would not need all this space in the entrance. That we should put a cabinet or two there.'

'The space is meant to let the customer catch a breath, rather than the whole thing jumping on them in one go. It should almost be like foreplay,' Karen said, wondering if foreplay was a good word to use with Gabrielle. She tried to steer her away from the topic. 'How are we going with the photographs for the lift?' she asked her.

'I have some delightful ones. I went through the ones in the album here and I have some of my own, all the way up until I left. There's one of me with Lauren Bacall, poor love. The book's over there, we'll look in a moment. I still don't understand this empty space and foreplay.'

'There will be the pictures we shot for the new Hamiltons fragrance, blown up to beyond life-size.

They should dominate the eye as you walk out of the lift. Imagine you're just coming out of the doors,' Karen said, turning with her back to them.

The plan was to have a blank space, almost like a waiting room, that restricted the overall view of The Garden until the customer rounded the corner and was faced with the whole thing, spread out before her. To Karen, it had to feel like entering an exhibition at an art gallery, passing through a small and minimal space and into something much bigger. It would create a sense of anticipation.

'So,' she said to Gabrielle, placing a hand on her shoulder, getting her first feel of the now familiar crushed velvet, today's colour being green, 'you come through the door, big picture of Maxwell and the doves curving over this low dome ceiling and the other two pictures on the side. Then you go through and you see a whole range of fragrances. It's familiar, because we don't want to shock or turn people off. It's what they would expect to see.'

She led Gabrielle into the empty space, trying to create for her the image of what was to come.

'You come through the entrance hall and there's a long red carpet held down by brass runners with potted palms at the side. Along either side, counters. Here,' she pointed to her right, 'will be shoes and hats and over there on the other side, lingerie. Through here, the next section, will be a range of select designers. Donna Karan, Chanel, Vivienne Westwood, Versace and some others, preferably English and perhaps just starting up. We'll switch them around every few months. There'll be plants along some of the walkways and in corners and in high hanging baskets. This is where the fountain and bar will be.' They had reached the central point.

'Over there, the juice bar,' she pointed to it, already constructed around the plumbing for the fountain which protruded from a plinth. 'Over that side, on those counters will be some jewellery and other accessories. As you pass the bar and fountain, there is space for more women's wear. And there on the back wall,' she pointed dramatically, 'will be a high wall with water cascading down it very discreetly. Like the Trump Plaza in New York, but not as garish. The water wall will gently cascade and the gantry you see up there will be open too, allowing you to go up and be near the flow of water and to see The Garden from an ariel perspective. Sofas are going to be spread about, staff able to assist if you need it. Don't you think this will be a wonderful place to come and shop?'

'Perhaps. I really think there should be something more outside the lift,' Gabrielle said, as though all Karen had just said to her was meaningless. 'Some people to greet the customers? Handsome men or something?'

'Definitely not. Cliché. That was discussed at the original meeting and subsequently with Daniel. The photographs will be enough. The green marble on the floor, the gold trim around the edges. It will all carry itself off. Why don't you show me those pictures now?'

Karen spent half an hour looking through the Hamiltons collection and Gabrielle's personal collection of photographs. She may not have particularly liked her, but the pictures were interesting and she felt a little sorry for the woman, her collection of memories mounted in a book and yellowing slowly around the edges.

'Is that Alan?' Karen exclaimed at one point.

'Oh yes. Quite the looker wasn't he? A very popular man with the staff in his younger days, especially the young ladies. Look, this is a ball we had in the Christmas of nineteen-sixty-seven. Alan would have been, oh, twenty-two. Only just joined and Daniel too, his father still here. Look, that's Lawrence Avendon.'

'He'd divorced your mother by then?'

'Oh yes! They had not been together for over fifteen years by then. She was festering away in some nursing home or other. There she is.'

154

Gabrielle handed her a picture. A handsome woman, not pretty, with slightly frizzy hair, stared at the camera, a smile not quite breaking across the square features. Karen looked at it in silence, uncertain of what to say. Gabrielle seemed to be off in one of her customary orbits and Karen waited politely for her to land.

'She was very pretty,' Karen said.

'Not quite the belle, but near enough,' she replied.

By the time Gabrielle had finished showing her the photographs they ended up agreeing on several pictures that would be excellent. Karen turned and took another look at the area where The Garden was growing and then she made her way to find Caroline.

'Patisserie Valerie,' Karen said to the taxi driver as Caroline jumped in and she followed.

'How's the skirt holding up under the pressure?' Karen asked.

'I gave up with it by ten and just hiked it up under my ears.'

'How's Daniel been?'

Caroline took a deep breath. 'He's very charming, you know. That view from his office and the meeting room is amazing. You wouldn't think you could see that much from there.'

'Don't let him be too charming. Are you getting on okay with Jane?' The taxi rounded the corner of Knightsbridge and sped on past Harrods.

'She's lovely. She showed me where everything needed to go and left me to it, said I should just ask as many questions as I want. She's been there years.'

'There are a few like that at Hamiltons,' Karen said. 'There was this kind of Royal Family that existed at the start and they've stayed. Jane is one of them. Alan another.'

'You soon,' Caroline said. 'Queen Karen of Hamiltons. Duchess of The Garden.'

Karen cringed and paid the taxi driver.

155

'How was your morning?' Caroline asked her as they neared the front of the queue for a table. Karen drank in the bustle of customers and waiters around her. It was one of her favourite venues for lunch, just continental enough to afford a brief escape from the shop and the sandwich bar jungle that was the alternative.

'A bit fraught. Gabrielle – the one I told you about – was squabbling with the foreman of the shopfitters. I don't know if she's deliberately obstructing me or just showing early onset of Alzheimer's.'

'Don't be wicked, Karen.'

'It's true though. She just blasts off into space. I'm waiting for her to dock with the mother ship.'

'Can I come and see where they're doing the building?'

'Of course. You can come to the party as well,' Karen said as they made their way to the table.

'Is it all women?' Caroline asked, her eye-line following one of the waiters.

'No. Mixed that night. One chance for the boys to see what they're missing. Apart from the ones who are going to work there. We've recruited ten people internally, all women, for the launch and they're looking for the rest through agencies.' Karen scanned the menu, despite knowing already that she would order the vegetarian club sandwich. 'We're going to have a dry run with the staff teams in two weeks' time.'

Caroline ordered the same as Karen and when the waiter had left, she put her hands on the table in a serious pose and looked at Karen.

'Don't be annoyed with me,' she said.

'Why?' Karen asked.

'I spoke to Gareth.'

'Today?'

'Just before you came up.'

Karen sighed, knowing that Caroline would do it despite all she had said.

'Don't tell me. He's sorry?' Karen raised her eyes sarcastically.

'He hasn't made it that far yet,' Caroline said. 'He's still denying that he went away with her. I told him I'd called Marilyn's work and his. He got really angry.'

'Did you tell him you were staying with me?'

'No. He wouldn't even think of you. If he did, I don't think he'd remember where you work or live. He couldn't remember where I worked, half the time.'

'We might have to give him that one, Caroline. I couldn't keep up with that. How did you leave it with him?'

'I didn't. I told him that I just called him to let him know that I was all right and that I wouldn't be back. We were supposed to go to his sister's wedding next month and that's all he seems to be worried about – what his family will think.'

'You're not going back to him, are you, Caroline?'

'No. Promise,' Caroline replied immediately.

Karen remembered how she had felt the night she drove with Caroline and rescued all her stuff. It had not seemed like a place where a couple lived. It had taken just less than two hours to pack and remove all of Caroline's things from his house. Karen had felt it should take longer to disentangle yourself from someone you were supposed to be living with. Instead, all of Caroline's things had stood out for her the second she walked into the house. Karen would not let her go back.

'I saw Alan Saxton,' Caroline said.

'What did you think of him?'

'Very sexy. I know what you mean about a cabinet minister. He looks so solid, and he's got that sort of magnetism. Daniel's like that too. What's Richard like?'

'He's very young and trendy. Go down and look at him in the Dungeon.'

'How will I recognise him?'

'He's the cutest and straightest thing Hamiltons has down there.'

'Which of them do you prefer?'

'To be truthful, and selfish, I'd prefer them both, but that's starting to be difficult. Not so much with Richard. I know he plays around a bit, but with Alan it's hard. He was knocked back by the divorce and I don't want to hurt him all over again.'

'What do you think he'd say if he knew about Richard?'

'He'd be terribly understanding, stiff in the upper lip, but I'm sure, at the centre of it, he'd feel devastated. He may find out anyway. I think the grapevine is running in overdrive through the shop.'

'Better he hears it from you,' Caroline said.

'I don't agree. In some ways, I'd sooner he hears it through gossip.'

'So you're just going to sit tight and let it work itself out?' Caroline asked, sounding unconvinced.

'I intend to do just that,' said Karen as she took a bite from the sandwich, unaware that even as she spoke, things were working themselves out and in a far stranger way than she could have imagined.

Chapter Fifteen

'IS THIS THE room for the interview?'

Karen looked up from the papers on her desk to be confronted by the toothy smile of a young man, probably not twenty, with long black hair that drooped in a fringe and a sculpted face that was long in lines and hard on edges. It was David's day off, which was why the boy must have ambled into her office in the way he had, and Karen was quick to capitalise on it as her mind quickly rehearsed a few lines.

'There are a number going on today,' she said, trying to sound severe and businesslike. 'Who are you?'

'Glenn Carpenter. It's for the part-time job on men's fragrances.'

'Come on in. My name's Karen Taylor. I look after recruitment here,' she lied quickly and efficiently, smiling as she slowly reeled him in.

Ordinarily, Stephen Jones, Hamiltons' personnel officer, would weed through the casual staff, but Karen saw a chance to add something special to the situation and take some workload from Stephen. She was nothing, she thought frivolously, if not a company woman. She stood and shook hands with him, crossing the room to click the door silently so he would not be aware that she was locking the both of them in. She was quickly excited and when she returned to her chair, she sat with her legs positioned so that she could move them slightly and cause the gentlest of friction between them.

He was well over six feet tall, but there was nothing skinny about him, all the signs of a good body hiding under the smart but casual clothes. His eyes were large and round, a very inviting shade of green, and his mouth was wide and pouting, giving the overall impression of an endearing gawkiness and almost shyness. He was very manly despite his youth and wouldn't stand a chance with the boy-kittens on the men's fragrances, but she didn't want to tell him that just yet. Why shatter the poor boy's illusions, she thought to herself? She picked up the first piece of paper that came to hand and pretended to study it before looking up at him.

'Tell me something about yourself, Glenn,' she said to him, moving her right leg from side to side, the back of her thigh rubbing the chair.

'Well,' he stumbled, 'I'm eighteen and I just finished my A' Levels, but I'm not going to university until next year, so I want to do some part-time work while I wait. It's sort of meant to be a year off, so I'm only looking for part-time.'

His accent had the trace of a good school, probably not public, but certainly private. Karen imagined him playing sports, mud covering his muscular legs, sweat on his brow, communal bathing. She brought her legs together and squeezed them, as though trying to smother her desire.

'What are you going to study when you get to university?'

'History, most likely. Unless I end up not going at all and just going to work.' He looked at her and she could tell he felt he had been too candid with her.

'You really should go to university. It's an eye-opener, if nothing else, and you've got plenty of time to go to work. Enjoy yourself.' She regarded him with a close gaze.

'I've worked in a shop before, on a Saturday. It was a chemist's, so I've dealt in aftershaves and things before.' He was quickly volunteering the information and seemed confused that Karen had gone into a wistful recollection of her college days and had not asked him any proper interview questions.

'How long did you work at the chemist?' she asked, her right hand disappearing discreetly under her desk, the thumb hovering over the material of her skirt.

'Six months,' he said to her, appearing to get into some sort of question-answering mode that his careers officer had probably shown him.

'Did you operate a till, process credit-card transactions, that sort of thing?'

'Yes, all of that, and sometimes I would advise people on what brand of aftershave or perfume to buy – people who were buying presents usually.'

'What's your favourite aftershave?' she asked him, hoping it would seem relevant.

'Armani,' he said and then added an after-thought: 'It's lovely.'

'Favourite woman's perfume?'

'That new Donna Karan is different. It almost smells like new suede.'

She smiled, wondering if he had rehearsed these answers, actually thinking someone would ask him what his favourite fragrances were. She had run out of things she could ask him and decided it was time to ask the important questions.

'Do you have a girlfriend, Glenn?'

'Not at the moment,' he answered awkwardly, a trace of suspicion in his voice.

'A boyfriend?'

'No,' he strained, as though all the air had been slowly syphoning from the room throughout their conversation.

'But you'd quite like to fuck me, wouldn't you?'

He stared at her in silence, the question appearing to fly at him like a jab, knocking him over and leaving him reeling.

'Don't worry,' she said, 'it's not an interview

question.'

Still the silence persisted and Karen was afraid he might burst as he sat there, his features all going awry and his skin reddening.

'I'm serious,' she said to him. 'Would you like to fuck me? I bet you read about this sort of thing all the time. Well, now's your chance to make it happen. Would you like to fuck me?'

'I . . . uh . . . I . . .'

'Glenn, I'd like to fuck you, I'll be honest. There's no point in messing about.'

'Here?' he asked her, and she knew she had him, and so did her pussy as it tightened between her legs ready to spring into action.

'Unless you have somewhere else in mind. The window-ledge?'

Karen eyed him and then with a single and dramatic motion of her arm, she swept her desk clean. All her papers, the phone, her calculator and her mobile phone crashed to the floor in a cacophony, Glenn looking around all the while as though he expected someone to burst in on them. Cleared of everything, the desk looked bigger and much more inviting. The blinds were pulled and tilted just enough to allow sunlight in but nothing else – certainly not any prying eyes from across the square. She stood up to go round the desk and he stood also.

'Stay,' she said shortly, and he fell back into his chair.

She sat on the edge of her desk, less than a foot from him, and ran her eyes over him. A green plaid shirt, very Ralph Lauren, and a pair of bottle-green chinos, even more very Ralph Lauren. He wore Timberland shoes and green socks that matched his shirt, an obvious attempt at co-ordination for the purposes of interview.

Karen put one foot either side of him on the edge of his chair, her skirt falling into the hollow of her legs. She inhaled, as though she were a conductor wielding a baton before an enormous orchestra, and she concentrated hard. While he looked on, Karen gently moved the skirt over her crotch, the sound of fabric on fabric filling the small space between them. She pushed her feet into the sides of the chair, the insteps of her shoes touching the outside of his bum on each side and it felt tight. He held her legs and his palms made cups around her calves, squeezing them with a forcefulness and passion.

As she let her head fall back a degree, she hitched the skirt up, pulling her legs back from him a fraction and lifting them. The skirt fell back against her to reveal white panties. His eyes lit and she saw him skip a breath, his own need now evident from the distended state of the front of his chinos. Karen circled her finger over the white cloth where it covered her smouldering sex. The crotch of her knickers was warm and a moistness was seeping through from the inside to the out. She kicked off each of her shoes in turn. With her bare right foot, she explored the front of Glenn's trousers, not having to search too far for the expected hardness.

After she had toyed with him just enough, she re-positioned her legs and turned her attention back to herself. She shifted the mound of her pussy back and forth under her own insistent and attentive touch, carefully kindling as though she were nursing a very delicate instrument in her hands which would gradually assume a much more menacing and forceful hunger to which they would both yield. The tip of her thumb concentrated in the vicinity of her clitoris, which rose and swelled as if it were trying to break through the soft damp fabric that arrested its development. Karen pushed her thumb into the elastic on the leg and ran it up her slit, pushing it aside and sliding easily up the well-lubricated pathway, attacking her clitoris from underneath before withdrawing the digit.

'Why don't you take them off?'

It was Glenn, bug-eyed and breathing fast.

'Why don't *you* take them off?' she replied immediately.

He leaned forward in the chair and she listened to the sound his behind made against the shiny blue leather as he reached for her knickers. Karen placed a hand either side of her on the edge of the desk and raised her bottom as Glenn whisked her panties down with the sort of speed and enthusiasm that only an eighteen-year-old could manage. Richard would have been too busy reading the label on her panties rather than staring at her pussy in the way Glenn was at that moment, fascinated and as though he were looking over the edge of some precipice, instinctively drawn towards it. Karen continued to raise herself up, hands on the desk and feet on the chair, arching her back and pushing herself up towards him, tantalising him. She dropped her behind, sitting on the edge of the desk so her legs hung over it and Glenn abruptly stood and pushed himself against her.

As he kissed her, his hands rode her skirt up around her hips and toyed with them and the outsides of her thighs, gradually encircling and approaching her where she most wanted him to. She wrapped her legs around him and squeezed him into her, the cotton feel of his chinos silken against her bared pussy, the hardness of an eager and youthful cock scarcely concealed by it. With haste, she pushed him away and undid his trousers in her favourite zipper, belt and button combination, eyeing his legs as they were revealed from under the descending trousers. He wore loose boxers of a blue denim material that had been washed to a delicate fade, a dark damp patch visible on the otherwise pristine surface of them. She felt the top of his bum just protruding from the boxers as she ran her fingers over the waistband and she pushed her hand in, feeling the warmth and the taut smoothness of one of his buttocks, the sensation sending a deep-seated spasm through her as the lust took hold.

She held him tightly as they covered each other in

hot panting breaths and she whispered hotly into his ear, 'What would you like to do to me, you dirty boy?'

He ignored her and continued to nuzzle at her collar-bone and the part of her neck that was exposed from beneath her blouse.

'There must be something,' she whispered, wondering suddenly if he was a virgin, although doubting that a cute boy like this could be at his age.

'What?' she said, not hearing him when he mumbled against her ear.

'I'd like to spank you,' he whispered, avoiding her eyes.

Karen frowned to nowhere or no one in the room, slightly taken aback by his forwardness and the timorous way he couched it. An order barked in a whisper. She pushed him back and looked at him and he had trouble meeting her gaze, obviously embarrassed. Karen turned, hitched her skirt up around her waist and bent over the edge of her desk.

His request may have been timid but once she was over the desk, he seemed to find an assurance that had escaped him previously. She felt him grip the back of her skirt and jerk it, exposing her rear fully, and then he gave it a solid and firm slap that had a gentle weight behind it. As the hand landed, it caused a ripple in her behind and the warmth quickly spread under where he had left his palm. It was not a hard slap and there was no pain as such, only something more pleasurable. Karen stretched her arms and held on to the sides of the desk, raising herself on tiptoes and making the flesh of her buttocks taut. The next smack was quicker, a faint whistle as his hand travelled through the air, and then a sharp crack that was again square on the centre of her bottom.

Against the solid wooden edge of her desk, Karen's pussy was lifted by the ridge, and as he spanked her, she was pushed against it with just enough force to make her squirm. Soon her rear end began to tingle and heat up. She knew he would be able to see her pussy from behind, pouting invitingly, and she hoped it would entice him. His left hand was still holding up her skirt and the right was now fondling her and soothing the fire he was creating on her cheeks and the wetness he was causing between her legs. After his hand rained on her several times, she felt the zip and buttons on her skirt being undone and then it was removed from her.

For a second or two, he was not touching her and she heard him remove his underwear. From behind, the smooth head of an unfamiliar cock explored her pussy-lips, tracing up and down them, hot hard flesh against soft lubricated folds of skin. As the head of it parted her, fluid escaped and she gripped the edges of the desk tighter. While his cock was delving, his hand slapped down and caught her on the top of her buttock, obviously falling from above rather than directly from behind as it had done previously. He had pushed her blouse up and her back was exposed, his hands gently caressing it and rubbing the skin as though applying talcum powder. Every now and then, the softness and intimacy of the gesture would be broken by a strike to her behind. Karen enjoyed the switches between gentle and firm, his hand teasing her and then rudely awakening her. She waited for the moment when his probing cock would stir her in the same fashion and gripped on to the desk in anticipation.

A finger, his index, popped itself slyly inside her. More deft and agile than the cock, it probed her pussy, searching her lips and entering her vagina, the walls yielding wetly to it. His finger tested her, gauged her depth and flexibility as it penetrated her, the side to side movements of it causing her to cry out for the cock that would fill her. The shape and the crook of his finger felt larger than they were, the sensitivity of her vagina magnifying their size. The sensation of pleasure it created in her felt like a noise that was slowly growing louder and louder, reaching a din that would deafen her.

'I want to see you fuck me,' she said to him, the words

issuing from her suddenly, the finger in her hesitating and then withdrawing.

Karen stood upright, removed her blouse and bra, and turned naked to face him. He stood, hands hanging loosely at his sides and cock protruding from under his shirt. His legs were muscular and well shaped, like a runner's or a cyclist's. She approached him and gently undid his shirt, starting with the buttons on the cuffs and then running from the neck downwards. As she removed his shirt, he was kicking off the Timberlands and working his trousers and underwear off his ankles. When they were both naked, he reached and fondled her breasts, tweaking at the nipples. She looked at his own nipples, small and hard circles on his defined chest.

She gripped his cock and exerted pressure on it, feeling it pulse in her hand, and then she worked his foreskin back and forth, his own fluid making the action slick and hot. The size and heat of it were perfect and she masturbated him gently as she imagined the feel of his bone-like member burrowing into her, propelled by the force of his enthusiastic and youthful body. Already she envisioned his orgasm, the tight and circumscribed nature of it as he released himself so precisely and agonisingly into her, his cock palpitating inside her and his semen spurting deeply, his whole body racked by the effort required to bring him to that point. She looked at him and imagined it all, saw it foreshadowed in the studious and concentrated manner of his face as she manipulated him with her fingers.

The desk was firm against her back. Karen lay with her feet over the edge and she re-positioned herself several times before she was happy with the position of her body and the angle at which she would be able to receive Glenn as he stood and thrust into her. Her recently spanked bottom was on the edge of her desk and her pussy was up at almost the perfect height for Glenn to crouch slightly and enter her, which, with little ceremony or delay, he did.

Karen lifted her head and watched him, wanting to see what was responsible for the delightful invasion she was feeling. She revelled in his face, a mixture of attention and reverie, and she felt completely taken by him, in his image and his physical nature. The cock which she had been handling only moments earlier was now passing through the lips of her pussy. As it made its slow and aching journey, she dropped her head back, the vision of him, his strong torso tensing and his long hair falling into his face, still imprinted on her mind. He put his hands on to her pelvis and came to rest against her, his balls against her. A long and noisy sigh escaped her and she realised that she had been holding her breath all the while he had penetrated her. Now, as though to make room for him in her, she was exhaling. She rippled herself around him and allowed her legs to part wider.

With a definite and positive stroke, he fucked her. If this had been Richard or Alan, she would have thought they were making love. But here was an eighteen-year-old who had mistakenly wandered into her office and with whom she had flirted and then been spanked by as she bent over her desk. What they were doing now, quite simply, was fucking – and Karen was loving every moment of it. Each lunge he made into her and the animalistic sound that accompanied it. The breach he made into her and the way it threw her pussy into a tumult left her with nowhere to hide from him as he found new depths and different speeds and intensities with which to reach them. Karen lay back and let him do the work, her own hand occasionally wandering to her clitoris to comfort it.

The force of his movements pushed her up and down the surface of her desk, her back moving an inch or two against the grained leather of the inset. Her toes just touched the floor, pointed towards it like a ballet dancer about to pirouette. As his cock drove home, her toes left the floor for a second before dropping back to make a soft contact with the carpet. His hips and pelvic area felt hot and sweaty as they banged into her and, as his body slapped against hers, a dull thud issued from the point of contact. She was driven back by the thrust, her legs opening slightly wider each time, roused from their gently dangling position.

Karen was impressed and surprised at his stamina, having braced herself for a somewhat quicker experience. The continued and methodical nature of his technique was exciting as she felt herself gradually lose all method and control of her own, ready to explode in a confused and disorganised frenzy. Against his ordered pattern she would offer abandon and offer to take him there with her.

Although she could not put a time on it, Karen imagined he must have been there for almost ten minutes, the hard cock in the soft warm depths. She sensed he was close to relinquishing the grip he had kept on his desire for so long, as though he had been holding his breath in the same way she had earlier as he had entered her. The fucking became more intense, a deep fervour holding them both and surrounding their bodies in a kind of heat that bound them together.

His orgasm was as she had imagined it earlier. The continuity of his movements was gone and he surrendered to it as he jerked and snatched his body upwards as though trying to lift himself off the ground. His hair flicked wildly around his face which was a contorted scowl of elation and the muscles in his shoulders and upper arms tensed and un-tensed in time with his flow into her. He yelped helplessly, on display for her and unable to hide his feelings. His semen was warm as it shot into her in several short pulses. She imagined the head of his cock, the eye opening as it forced his come from deep in him, flooding her pussy. As he came, he continued to jog his cock in her pussy, the movements much shorter and erratic. When he withdrew, she looked up and saw his pubic hair matted with juices, his cock slicked with a shining film and its head displaying a pearl of his semen.

Breathing heavily, his cock still juddering, Glenn reached down and set to work on her. He masturbated her furiously and she felt his come inside of her as he centred on her clitoris, every now and then pushing a finger into her. She shifted her gaze between his hand and his face, transfixed by what he was doing to her. Her orgasm was moments away, her rear was still warm from the spanking and her pussy still reverberating from the presence of his cock. Now, with his finger, he was finishing what she had started. In a gentle swell, she felt the climax stir inside, relieved that she was so close and already wistful at the thought that it would soon be over.

Her orgasm galvanised her; vagina moving power-fully and of its own accord, Karen subordinated to its movements and the willing victim of the wave it sent through her. She rocked and squirmed against the desk. As Glenn's hand practically grasped at her, it was as if he were trying to hold on to her very self, preventing her escape. She clung to the orgasm as if she had her arms around it and was slowly letting it release. The movements of his fingers produced stimulation in a way Karen was barely aware of. She balanced off the edge of the desk in a breathless daze.

'Is this the room for the interview?' he asked her again.

Karen wondered how long the fantasy had taken and for what length of time she had sat at her desk, staring through him and projecting his image in her mind.

'Come on in,' she said to him, standing and adjusting her skirt.

Chapter Sixteen

'WHAT TIME'S HE coming?' Caroline asked her.

Karen checked her watch. It was seven-forty.

'At eight-thirty – there's no "about" with Alan. It will be eight-thirty exactly.'

Karen fitted her earring and flicked her hair with her hand, shaking her hair and letting it settle naturally.

'I don't know why you changed. You looked fine as you were,' Caroline said, appraising her thoughtfully.

'That was my interview suit,' she told her.

'For the media, you mean?'

Karen had been interviewed by one of the Sunday supplements in connection with The Garden and with the Hamiltons fragrance. It was a useful piece of free publicity and she had given little away in the interview, hoping that what detail she did give would entice women to come along. Several of the papers were going to cover the launch party and several had been pointedly refused access.

'Exactly. For the good lady of the press. How do I look?'

'You look fine. I haven't seen you this jumpy since . . . well, ever, I suppose. This is the first time he's ever been here?' Caroline asked, though she knew the answer.

'Yes. And the last. I feel awful about this, but I think it's going to be the best way.' Karen looked at herself in the mirror, hoping her YSL trouser suit had the requisite proportions of hardness and homeliness she felt the task would require. A bitch in couture was better than a bitch in nothing at all.

'You know best. He seems like a nice guy, very polite. He spends a lot of time with Daniel.'

'Caroline, do you flutter your eyelids like that when Avendon is actually there? This is a bit schoolgirl, you know? I'll tell Daniel you're on Prozac if you like.'

Much to Karen's somewhat guilty surprise, the job she had arranged for Caroline at Hamiltons had worked out well. Caroline was enjoying it, simpering on about Daniel, using it as a way of relieving the monotony of filing, and Daniel seemed to like her. She wondered what would happen when the project was over. There was not a place for Caroline in The Garden and Karen had been keeping it from her that the auditions, as they were being called, had already happened for the women. They were left looking for five token men and that would happen the next day.

'Of course I don't flutter at him. Anyway, I'll make myself scarce.'

'Are you sure you don't mind?'

'Karen, it's your flat. I'm going to see a few of the girls from one of my old jobs. I'll be fine and I'll have more fun than you by the sound of it.'

'Promise me you're not sneaking off to see Gareth.'

'Karen. I won't be back until late.'

There was a buzz on the doorbell and they both froze and looked at each other, uncertain of what to do. Karen realised how jumpy she was. It normally took more than a doorbell to put her off her stride.

'Is it him?' Caroline asked.

'Too early for Alan,' Karen said, composing herself and going to the entry-phone.

'Delivery for Miss Taylor,' a voice crackled.

'Come on up,' she said, buzzing the front door.

It was a huge arrangement of orchids. Karen thanked the delivery boy and closed the door.

'Who are they from?' Caroline asked, sounding

curious and excited at once.

Karen looked at the card and smiled, handing it to Caroline who read it out.

'I'm in town next week and wondered if there was going to be a sequel to our movie. Do I at least get invited to the party? Chris N.' Caroline looked at her. 'Who's Chris N?'

'Somebody I met in New York, a friend of a friend.'

'Hmm. And does he get an invite to the party? You'll be a free agent again by then, won't you?' Caroline said.

'All being well,' Karen said, the first smattering of doubt staining her resolve.

When she had gone, Karen started to wish Caroline had stayed a while longer. She did not relish the prospect of fidgeting for the next thirty-five minutes while she waited for Alan to arrive. She quickly arranged the flowers in one of her many oversized and normally unused vases and was about to fix herself a drink when the buzzer rang. Only eight o'clock. She buzzed the building front door and waited for the knock on her front door, going to the fridge while she did.

'Hi.' It was Richard. He walked casually in, kissing her on the cheek on his way past.

Karen shut the door and quickly said to him, 'What are you doing here? I thought you were at a party at the gym?'

'I didn't fancy it. I wanted to see you. The pant-suit is very retro, by the way. Nice. YSL?'

She ignored him, flustered and angry. She had twenty-five minutes to get rid of him, but he had already planted himself on the sofa and did not look likely to move in any short space of time. She checked her watch, the second hand seeming to have trebled its speed, and she thought of Alan on his way to see her. This would not be a pretty scene at all.

'Let's do something really horny,' she said to him, her mind finding a foothold.

'Like what?' he asked her, a willing grin on his face.

She grabbed his hand and pulled him off the sofa,

173

dragging him down the hall, ignoring her own bedroom, and on into Caroline's room. She took his linen jacket off and unbuttoned the shirt, still managing to notice in the rush that it was Comme des Garçons. She told him to kick off his shoes and then popped the buttons on the fly of his Katharine Hamnett jeans and took him out of them and his 2XisT underwear. She decided to leave his socks on.

'I'll be right back. Lie down,' she said to him.

Scrabbling in the wardrobe of her own bedroom, she found what she was looking for and returned.

He looked at her with surprise as she produced a pair of handcuffs. She had bought them from a tacky tourist shop in Oxford Street.

'This is interesting,' he said, as she clicked one of the bracelets shut on his wrist and brought his hands up to thread the cuffs through the brass bedstead before locking his other wrist in.

'It gets better,' she said, making several small knots into one large ball at the centre of an Hermès scarf. She pushed the knot into his mouth and tied the gag gently at first, gradually pulling it tighter. She put her finger to her lips, indicating for him to be quiet. As a final touch, she placed a blindfold on him, the one from the courtesy kit given to her on the flight to New York. She looked at him, his naked virile body locked to the spare bed, gagged and blindfolded, the blindfold bearing a single and inappropriate word. Virgin.

The gentle tumescence of his cock was an indication that he was finding the experience not unpleasant. She sat on the edge of the bed and touched him, squeezing and fondling his balls as she watched him become erect, looking at her watch as she did so. She pinched one of his balls and from behind the gag he gave a yelp. She brought her head down and breathed over his cock, letting the hot air from her mouth circulate around him. She blew, his pubic hair moving from the draught she created, but she did not touch his cock.

The doorbell rang. Richard tensed on the bed.

174

'Don't worry, I'll get rid of them,' she said, jumping off the bed and closing the door behind her.

The first time Alan had been early or late for anything, she thought to herself, buzzing the front door to let him in the building. She rearranged herself and waited. He knocked on the door.

'Hello,' he said to her cheerfully, flowers in hand.

'Oh darling, let's do something really dirty,' she said, grabbing him by the lapel and hauling him through the door.

Less than five minutes later, he was in her bedroom, tied to the headboard and gagged, another scarf making do as a blindfold.

It was going to be a double header.

'I'll be back,' she said to Alan.

Karen went to the kitchen and hastily gathered several items from the fridge. In the hallway, the doors of the spare room with Richard and her room with Alan across from each other, Karen removed all of her clothes and tried to decide which door to choose.

'Okay,' she said to Richard. 'Let's play.'

His cock was still quite firm, like his body, and she felt like jumping on top of it there and then and riding it. But she could not.

'I'm naked. And I have some presents for you. I'm going to give them to you one at a time and you have to be a quiet boy. Do you understand?'

He nodded obediently and she smiled, pulling the foil lid from a carton of peach yoghurt, low fat of course. She scooped some up in her fingers and slathered it over his cock, a thin layer making it glisten in the light of the room and the member hardening under her touch. He seethed from the coldness of it, moving his legs around, the muscles in them rippling as he did so, those on his arms taut from the position in which he was cuffed. She applied more to him and he became fully aroused. Greedily and quickly, she licked and sucked at him, the peach flavour of the yoghurt mingling with his own taste. Soon, his cock was bare once more, no trace of what had covered him only seconds earlier. He pushed his crotch upwards, imploring her for more.

'You need to cool off,' she said to him, picking an ice-cube from the bowl she had brought with her and quickly inserting it into his rear, the wetness providing its own lubrication. He whined and she leapt off the bed, leaving the room and crossing the hall.

'Now,' she said to Alan, 'we're going to play and you have to be a nice quiet boy, understand?'

With a similar obedience to Richard, he nodded. His cock was not as animated as Richard's had been. She would soon rectify that. She knelt between his legs and massaged him with her deft fingers, pulling his foreskin back and forth over the head of his cock, occasionally applying pressure. It enlarged with her gentle ministrations and she was not as rough or as quick as she had been on Richard. When he was full and ready, she opened the bottle of Absolut she had removed from the freezer, took a large swig and gargled with it, the heady liquid like ice in her mouth. She swallowed half of what was in her mouth, needing the alcohol, and quickly dipped her head down to suck him, not letting the remaining vodka escape.

His body twisted and writhed – the sensation must have been a mixture of cold and sharp, the temperature of the vodka so ice cold and the alcohol a stinging pleasure. She rinsed it around in her mouth, letting it wash around his cock, swishing it back and forth, the feel of it tingling in her mouth. She imagined how that must have translated to the delicate collection of nerve-endings on Alan's cock. She threw her head back and swallowed the last of the spirit and was then back on him, lathing at his shaft and taking him deep into her. She grabbed his ball sac and closed her hand around it, feeling how the testicles moved around and off each other.

'Hold tight and I'll be right back.'

There was a damp cold patch on the duvet beneath

Richard. His cock was still erect and he wriggled when he heard her enter, trying to say something. She told him to be quiet.

'Listen to me,' she said. 'Can you hear what I'm doing?'

He became very silent and very still on the bed, no further sounds coming from his mouth or from any movements of his body. The only sound left in the room was that of Karen's hand, insinuating itself into her pussy, parting the lips and directing its attention towards her clitoris. The sounds she made were delicious, a slow and wet labial rhythm, the inside of her vagina pulsing with an appetite for him. She looked at him and saw the strain his cock was under, pushed from the inside by the coursing of his blood. He began to move again, as though trying to compensate for his inability to touch himself and her lack of touch on him.

Karen climbed over him, resting her hands on his chest and straddling his groin, her pussy far from his cock. She sank an inch and then another inch. Still there was no contact between her pussy and his unyielding cock, but Karen could feel the heat transferring between their bodies. With great care and attention, as though trying to thread a needle, she lowered her body by the millimetre. Her warm lips just brushed the underside of his cock and she pulled back the instant he tried to move upwards towards her.

'That's not allowed,' she told him.

Again she dropped her body and allowed more and longer contact, but still only seconds in time and fractions of a touch. Richard snorted through his nose, sounding both inflamed and frustrated, his cock similarly angry and fit to burst. She skimmed her pussy-lips all the way along the underside of his shaft, his cock pressed solidly back against his stomach, supporting herself on her knees and arms as she did so. Her desire was now stronger than her need to tease him and she let the touch become heavier and the contact-time longer, using his cock to stimulate herself. She became wetter and her pussy felt heavier, pulled by gravity and by the lure of his cock. She was about to reach, hold him upright, and descend on to his shaft when she remembered Alan.

'I'm going to come back when you've calmed down and then fuck you stupid,' she whispered to Richard, ignoring the exasperated murmur that emitted from him.

In the hall, she paused for breath. What had started out as a game for her, a way of trying to keep the both of them happy, had now started to make its demands on her. Her pussy was alight with the urge to be penetrated and in her mind she anticipated the power of the orgasm she would be able to unleash if she could only spend long enough with either of them to get there. Of course, there being two of them presented the opportunity for her to do just that, twice.

'I'm naughty, don't you think, Alan? Getting you all hot and then running off and leaving you. I should be punished. There's a hairbrush on the dresser here, a nice round one.'

She picked it up and spanked it solidly against one of her buttocks, the stinging sensation spreading fast across the cheek. She applied it to herself several more times, getting the hang of it. She changed hands and chastised her other buttock, crying out in a small and coquettish voice, deliberately trying to excite Alan as he lay on the bed. It was working. He was clenching and unclenching his buttocks, the motion pushing his cock up in the air while his feet moved about restlessly on the bed.

When her backside was glowing from the self-inflicted paddling she had supplied with the hairbrush, she moved closer to the bed and inspected him. His body was exceptional for a man his age, the curve and line of it dense and masculine, the limbs sturdy. She rubbed herself, the need now strong. She could not wait any longer. She mounted the bed and him simultaneously and with little grace or aplomb, grabbed his cock and pushed it inside her. Her pussy was moist and ready, his member intimating itself into her with an ease that was a joy. Karen settled on to him, not stopping her descent until their bodies forced her to stop, joined at the groin.

With her hands on his sides, she moved furiously, using the spring of the mattress to give her the required leverage, the bed squeaking in a fast whine as she did so. She made no allowance for passion, that emotion having long since surrendered to simple and unbridled lust. She ground herself into him, feeling the rub of him against her, the walls of her vagina alive to the sensations it was giving her, her clitoris quivering. She forced him in and out of her with a motion that was unswerving and without compassion for him or his needs. Karen enjoyed using him like this and knew she would return to him and finish him off when she was ready.

Her orgasm came like a dream in the night; sudden and shocking, it roused her and sent signals all over her body. She wailed and threw her body about, arms flailing, but her pussy still firmly planted on Alan's cock, using it as a pivot, a stable point from which to release herself. The freedom of her movements and the liberation of the orgasm were contrasted by Alan, rooted to the bed and bound to it, unable to do much except give her pleasure. She used him for a while longer and then cruelly deprived him of her, lifting herself off and looking at the desperate and quivering member she left in her wake, already missing her pussy. He seemed almost resigned to his fate, as though he had caught on to the rules of the game.

She kissed him on the cheek, in the area of skin between the blindfold and the gag. 'I'm going to let you think about me for a little while,' she intoned breathily, 'and then I'm coming back to give you the orgasm of your life.'

'Show time,' she said to Richard. 'I need you harder

than that. Come on, imagine me here ready to sit on you. That's better, some signs of life down there.'

Richard was gritting his teeth around the gag, his arms straining against the cuffs, as he forced his cock to become erect of its own accord. Karen watched, fascinated by the way it changed size before her very eyes like a magic trick. Her pussy was still ringing from her orgasm, the force of it echoing through her. It was good to have a hard cock in front of her and one in reserve in her own bedroom.

Karen squatted over Richard, one hand on his chest and the other lifting his cock. She rested his phallus at the opening of her vagina, letting it just wait there as she anticipated the feel of it. As always, the anticipation was sweet but the reality of the penetration was sweeter. She took him into her, made him a part of her by allowing him access to her deepest and most intimate space as though she were sharing it with him. His cock was desperately hard, its length and width perfectly expanding and plumbing her. Riding him slowly at first, she tantalised him and herself. Richard started to groan virtually as soon as he was inside her, small sob-like sounds that were pleading with her to release him from the most important shackle of all and allow him to come. Massaging her clitoris with adept fingers, Karen brought herself as near to the edge as she could without toppling over it and going into free-fall, trying to time herself with him.

Speeding up her lunges on to him and on the caress of her clitoris, she felt her second orgasm fill the tracks of the first. Where the first had boiled over, the second was from deeper within, shaking her at the foundation and making her dizzy. She made less noise, keeping it to and for herself, balling the pressure up and then letting it release in carefully timed bursts, oblivious to Richard and to the room around her. Bound and gagged by her own passion, she was both its prisoner and its guard, alternating between tightly controlled sensations and untrammelled pleasure.

When she heard him shout from behind his muzzle, she slipped him out of her and masturbated him with a cruel and heartless slowness, prolonging the agony for him. His whole body froze and seemed to bury itself into the mattress as though a large invisible weight were bearing down on him. The weight of his orgasm. As the first shot of semen left him, Karen discarded his cock and left him to it. He threw his head from side to side and writhed, arching his back up off the bed and twisting his torso before finally banging his rear up and down off the bed, desperate to try and continue ejaculating unaided by her and pushed only by himself. It was agonising even to watch and Karen quietly left him as he covered his stomach with his own semen.

With Alan, she was kinder. With a tenderness and a care that was a complete contrast, she held Alan in her hands and stroked and rubbed him. It was a pleasant way to come down from her own orgasms, to gently bring Alan to one of his own. Karen reached out with a thumb and two fingers and held Alan. She pulled his foreskin as far back as it would go, making his glans look big as the blood pumped in. Moving her fingers up and down, the foreskin sliding back and forth, she masturbated Alan in a way that she was sure would be completely different to how he did it himself. She must have held his cock differently and moved it slower or faster than Alan would have. Perhaps the feeling of a different hand performing a task so familiar to him, the insistence of a rhythm so different from one that was naturally his own, would be like a drum with a new beat.

The semen flowed out of him like a small stream. Karen squeezed and let her fingers concentrate on moving his foreskin back and forth over his phallus. Rather than erupting from him, it seeped out and ran over her fingers. Clenching her whole hand around it, she felt the warm semen course over the back of her hand, a slightly white fluid with a familiar and exciting smell. The movements Alan made were tight and discreet, in keeping with the gentle ebb of his come, and Karen continued to grip and coax him until there was nothing left but the movement of her hand.

Sitting on the floor in the hallway, she was tired and spent. Two was fun, but it was hard work and she had not realised just how hard until that moment. Right there and then, in simple practical terms, Richard would be the easiest to get rid of, simply by telling him that getting dressed and leaving immediately was part of the high-class prostitute fantasy. She would return to him, wipe him down and put his underwear and trousers back on before freeing him. Easy. But she could hardly untie Alan and tell him that while she'd enjoyed herself, it was all over and could he please leave. Not least of all because she was not entirely sure she wanted him to leave.

Karen realised that she would have to make a choice and she would have to make it soon.

Chapter Seventeen

IT WAS TWENTY minutes after two in the afternoon and Karen was reluctantly admitting to herself that trying to find five men to act as staff in The Garden had not been as exciting as she had imagined. Twenty-five hopefuls, including ten from Hamiltons, had arrived at eight-fifteen that morning as instructed. Most had come from agencies and were a range of ages, all with the criterion that they were, or almost were, model handsome. Two or three others had come on recommendation, boyfriends of women or men at Hamiltons.

Group exercises and role plays were conducted, with Stephen Jones, the personnel director, organising, supervising and taking notes. He had gone on at Karen about psychometric testing and targeted selection, wanting to be even more involved than he was. Even to her untrained eye, it had been obvious to Karen who would be most likely to fit in with the spirit and atmosphere she was trying to create in The Garden. As she watched, so she had already formed some opinions about who would be the first to go and was secretly pleased when she found that her assessment agreed very closely with Stephen's. She had held firm over only one person, reminding Stephen first gently and then strongly that his role was advisory only. With him as advisor, Gabrielle as consultant and David as assistant, the whole Garden had become a juggling act. She watched David and Stephen conferring over something, their clipboards touching, and she sighed to herself. The last thing The Garden needed was men with clipboards. Just a while longer, she told herself, and then with The Garden up and running she would be able to rise above compromise.

One thing had surprised her. That Richard had shown almost no interest in working in The Garden. Looking at the twenty-five who had streamed through the door that morning, Karen was sure, even allowing for her bias, that Richard was far cuter than any of them. Karen could understand that he wanted to stay around men's clothes as they were very much his life and she also thought he did not like the idea of working directly for her. It was a shame he had not come along in any case as he may have been able to spice the auditions up slightly.

It had not been without event, though. Someone called Michael had marched in wearing full drag and a pair of stilettos which, along with his legs, Karen would have killed for. To a dumbstruck room he proudly announced, 'My name's Christie and I enjoy being a woman ... because I can.' Karen had to politely explain that they had found all the women they needed, only to be told Christie was, apparently, all the woman anyone needed. Several minutes of discussion, some of it quite political, had followed, and Michael/Christie had left happy, a point of some sort having been made. Perhaps when we've been running a few months and are successful, Karen thought to herself. She had been tempted to include him just to annoy Stephen, messing up all his little forms and quizzes.

It was when Karen and Gabrielle had whittled the twenty-five down to ten and David had asked her if there was going to be a swim-wear round that it occurred to Karen that the whole thing had gone from interview to audition to beauty pageant in fairly swift succession. David seemed to be having more fun than she and Gabrielle, herding the men around and giving them directions. The women had all been selected over a week earlier, including those who would act as team leaders. The five males would add some drapery, what David referred to as 'eye candy'. Karen was the only real judge as Gabrielle seemed indifferent to the process, sometimes asking a bizarre question that would floor someone completely, like the date of their mother's birthday. For Karen, it was the sort of situation where she would know what she was looking for once she saw it. All of the original twenty-five were perfectly fine, a good range of ages, colours and creeds, but she felt the need to make the selection based on more than just how good someone looked. Staff would be all important in The Garden.

The Garden would open in ten days' time. Most of the shop-fitting work had been done, with a few minor adjustments required, but everything else was sound and on time. Alan and Avendon had been impressed and Gabrielle, Karen noticed, had not been slow in trying to reflect as much of the glory as possible on to herself. Gabrielle was confusing, her attitudes ranging from passion for The Garden to disinterest in it, all the way to outright opposition.

The auditions were being held in The Garden itself, which looked like a skeleton with all the rails and cabinets empty of stock, the odd logo still to go on a wall. Karen and Gabrielle sat near the bar on plastic tables and chairs, the fountain installed but not yet running, using one of the areas that would hold women's designs to interview and talk to the candidates. An overhead projector and a screen had been set up for the afternoon and Stephen Jones was gone, his work accomplished. They had told everyone who was and was not being asked back after lunch and they readied themselves for the afternoon, waiting to whittle the ten down to five.

'Who do you want to see first?' David asked.

'Who would you pick first?' she asked him.

'Graham, definitely,' came an enthusiastic response.

'For the interview, I mean,' she intoned.

'Still Graham,' he smiled.

'Graham it is. Send him in.'

David went to fetch him and Karen looked over her notes and the CV and file she had been sent on Graham. He was thirty-three, tall, well-built and had modelled. With a degree in fashion and currently working a bar-job and a day-job in a shop, he was similar to everyone else, all looking to step up a rung from where they were. He had certainly made an impression on David, who had practically waltzed out of the room. Graham reminded Karen of the beefy black models Robert Mapplethorpe had photographed, with his well crafted features and hair cut close to his head.

'What did you think of this one?' Karen asked Gabrielle, making a token gesture towards her involvement in the process.

'He seemed very personable to me and attractive, but then all ten of them are attractive in their different ways. It's such a shame we couldn't employ them all.'

Each of the successful candidates from the morning had been given some blank transparencies and pens and told to come back after lunch and give a short five- to ten-minute presentation chosen from a list of subjects all related in some way to women's fashion. All twenty-five had been forewarned about it in the letters they received, so no one had any excuse, other than lack of interest, for not being prepared.

David lingered in the room for a second or two longer than he needed to, making a second unnecessary offer of coffee before leaving, Gabrielle seemingly oblivious to all around her. Karen wondered where Gabrielle went during these bouts of preoccupation.

'Graham, nice to see you again. Karen Taylor, and this is Gabrielle. I hope the fun and games this morning weren't too wearing?'

'No. I took a module at college on management and a

lot of the things this morning were familiar. I've done this sort of thing before.'

He had donned a pair of thin-framed tortoise-shell glasses that Karen did not remember seeing on him that morning and she was intrigued as to whether or not they had real lenses in them or were just ornamentation to make him look serious for the interview.

'Where did you model?' Gabrielle asked him.

'I did some catwalk at London Fashion Week two years ago and I've done some photographic for hair salons. Last time was for *Arena*, six months ago for a feature on suits. I'd tell you what month, but a feature on suits could be any month with them.'

'Obviously you've had a chance to read the covering information on The Garden and you heard the presentation this morning. Are there any immediate questions you have?' Karen asked him.

'There are a few, but why don't I do the presentation first and then we can talk afterwards,' he said, standing and producing slides. 'I've decided to focus on accessories, bags in particular . . .'

Graham's presentation came in at almost exactly ten minutes. He was knowledgeable and funny, a relaxed presenter who made Karen feel as at ease as he seemed to be. When he was done, they talked for twenty minutes, with an equal flow of questions, and Karen felt herself grudgingly acknowledge David's judgement, however different his motivations had been.

'Just finally,' Karen said. 'We've had these sniff cards of various different fragrances made up specially. They're all famous names, some men's and some women's. Just give them a smell and say which you think are for men and which are for women.'

'That simple?' he asked confidently.

He picked up a card and sniffed it. 'Polo Ralph Lauren, men.'

The next. 'Eternity, Calvin Klein, women.'

He tutted when he smelled the next card. 'Chanel

No. 5, please.'

'Oh, this is cheeky, it's Old Spice, isn't it. Men.'

After he had been through all eight cards and identified them by name, Karen had an impressed look on her face.

'You're not a perfumer in your spare time by any chance?' she asked, half-seriously.

'Fragrances are like a hobby for me.'

She handed him one final one and he raised it to his nose, concentrating hard.

'You've got me on this one. I don't know it,' he said eventually.

'Instinctively, would you say for a man or a woman, forgetting that you don't know who it's by.'

'Actually, it's hard to tell. I'm tempted to say either.'

He paused for a moment and a look of recognition seemed to dawn over his face.

'It's the new unisex one Hamiltons is launching, isn't it?' he said, eyeing her over the rim of the glasses.

Karen grinned.

'There was just one other thing,' she said. 'Can I try on your glasses? They're lovely.'

Obligingly and with a knowing smile he took them off and both he and Gabrielle stared at her as she put them on. She was able to see perfectly through the clear window glass. She took them off and handed them back, confident they were now looking for only four people from the nine that remained.

'Thanks for coming in,' she said. 'My assistant David will be in touch.'

'I liked him,' Gabrielle said, gazing at the empty shelves.

'So did I,' Karen responded encouragingly, unused to the feeling agreeing with Gabrielle gave her.

David came in with his clipboard and laid a sheet of paper on the table.

'I suggest you see them in this order,' he said.

'Does this mean they become progressively less cute?' Karen asked him wryly. 'After this morning they've all become a blur.'

'I think if you put all ten of them together you might get one good man,' he replied. 'Is the list okay?'

'Fine.' She studied it. 'Send Edwin in in about five minutes.'

When David had left the room, Gabrielle leaned towards her conspiratorially. 'I think your assistant may be gay,' she said gravely.

'Really?' Karen said, forcing her features to remain straighter than David. 'I'll keep that in mind.'

'Such a nice-looking boy . . .'

'Let's talk about Edwin,' Karen said, cutting Gabrielle off before she could say what a shame it was.

Edwin came and went with little fanfare or razzmatazz. He too had been a fashion student with some communication art thrown in, but apart from that, he was a world apart from Graham. Edwin was gawky and nervous. Obviously a better group performer, he had seemed much more impressive in the morning sessions. After he had left, Karen felt a tinge of worry. What if they were all like Edwin rather than Graham? Each one rejected stacked the odds; more to get from less. Then her rational mind took over. So what? They didn't really need the men anyway. Just see what comes along, window-shop a little.

They had seen two more people after Edwin, both of whom were suitable and they were in the middle of the presentation of the fifth person when David burst in, without his clipboard. Karen gave him an angry stare and the person presenting stammered and stopped. David made directly for Gabrielle and leaned over to whisper in her ear. Her expression went from benign to horrified, her mouth dropping and eyebrows raising, the skin seeming to tighten on her face for a long haggard second.

'Stop everything!' she shouted, standing abruptly and knocking over the chair.

'David, what is it?' Karen asked him.

'Daniel, Daniel!' Gabrielle cried out, not giving David a chance to speak. 'We will have to stop everything. At once. Oh my God.'

David put his arm around Gabrielle, who had begun to sob and shake. 'Daniel's had a heart attack,' he said to her. 'They've taken him away to hospital. It looked pretty serious according to Jane.'

'I didn't mean it. I didn't mean it, oh Daniel,' Gabrielle was mumbling through sobs.

'Can you look after her, David?' He nodded and led her away and out of the room, followed by the bemused eyes of the prospective employee who must have been wondering if this was part of the interview, some sort of initiative test.

Karen felt a throb in her left temple, a jolt of reality as she made hundreds of quick calculations about the situation, wondering what the effect would be. She guiltily ran the worst case scenario through her mind. Recovering, she thought about what she needed to do and what Avendon would do himself or want her to do. Show must go on, she heard him boom in the back of her mind. She turned to the man whose name she had completely forgotten, the short-term memory part of her brain fried by the sudden drama.

'Sorry. We've had a bit of a situation upstairs with a relative of hers. Can you pick it up from where you were?'

Chapter Eighteen

IT WAS THURSDAY night, late, and it was the eve of the opening party for The Garden. There would be a grand opening party on the Friday night and then doors would open for business on Saturday morning. Daniel Avendon had not been seen for the nine days following his heart attack, or what was being described as his 'heart episode'. It had not in fact turned out to be as bad as it had looked at the time. Karen had been told that the doctors were concerned and that he was under too much stress, things she would have expected to hear, but Daniel Avendon did not have a heart condition as such.

The mere mention of the words 'too much stress' had sent Gabrielle into a tail-spin of contrition. Her initial reaction at the day of the men's auditions had been to try and stop The Garden and possibly the whole of Hamiltons. Gabrielle seemed to feel that she may have caused Daniel's 'episode' by her own actions and she had been to spend time with him wherever he was hiding out and that had had the ultimate effect of convincing her that things must carry on unabated. Over the last nine days, Karen had seen very little of her and when she had, Gabrielle had not asked her a single question about what was happening with The Garden. Karen ended up having to chase Gabrielle for the photographs they were going to use for the lift. Alan had taken the helm in Daniel's absence and they had seen each other only once in the last ten days, both of them preoccupied by their own work. In sum, it was not how she imagined the day before The Garden would be.

'Is there anything else you want me to do?' David asked her, looking over a list on his clipboard. 'I've been through everything here, so unless anything else has cropped up . . . '

The day had been frantic. Karen had insisted that she did not want a mad rush on the final afternoon prior to the opening party. She had been through far too many similar situations with other promotions that she had worked on. She had reached a point, she realised, where that was not the sort of adrenalin she needed any more. That morning, there had been what seemed like a million people around, all seeking her attention, and as the day had progressed, the number of people interested in her had dwindled until she was left on her own, apart from David, loyal to the end.

'You know, I think we're pretty much set here. It's scary, isn't it? The number of promos we've been through where it's been insane and here we are, biggest project ever and it's going too well.' She looked around and then let her eyes fall on him. He looked tired.

'You're getting superstitious. Don't worry. I'm sure something will go at least a little bit wrong.' He paused. 'This is going to be great, you know that, don't you?'

From most other people she knew, Karen would have taken the comment cynically, but she looked at David, who was like an earnest little animal from a Disney film, and she knew he meant it.

'David, I couldn't have coped without you.'

'Karen, you're not going to sing, are you?'

They both burst out laughing, Karen enjoying the sound of it in the empty Garden, feeling the tension release from her.

'Okay,' she said. 'Enough of the mutual admiration

society. It's getting late.' She blinked and checked her watch. It was after ten. 'I have a date.'

'So do I,' David confided slyly.

'Really? I was starting to worry you might be neuter. You should have said. I didn't mean to keep you here so late.' —

'That's okay,' David said. 'It makes me look less keen that way.'

'Get out of here now,' she said to him. 'Are the flowers coming at three tomorrow?'

'Yes, after that weird balloon lady has finished. I can hold my own in a balloon discussion now. I know all about air-fill versus helium-fill.'

'It is going to be tasteful, David, isn't it? I don't want it looking like a birthday party at McDonald's.'

'Well, the balloon lady will be all right as long as we watch her and make sure she doesn't get carried away. I think she'd been on the helium when she came in last week.'

David left and Karen took a few minutes to walk around The Garden, drinking it all in like a final inspection. A captain touring the ship before some final battle. The lights seemed very bright to her tired eyes and she squinted. Karen had decided that The Garden should look ready for business when they had the grand opening party. That meant space was slightly more restricted than it might have been, but not by much, and that smoking would not be allowed at the party, which would be nicely controversial in a trivial way. She wandered through the different women's designs, the accessories section and around the bar and fountain. Continuing her backwards journey she passed more designs and was then on the long wide carpet in the entrance area, now fully lined with various palms and plants, gaps allowing people to jump off and into the lingerie or hat section. Standing in the entrance hall, she gazed up at the image of Maxwell that had been blown up to three times life-size and fitted around the false dome that had been created in the entrance, making him look like something from the Sistine chapel. Karen wished there was a light switch by the lift door that she could simply flick and all the lights would go off, giving it a sense of completeness and making it feel like it was all truly hers. The lift arrived and she left.

Richard was already at her flat when she arrived there. There was a smell of cooking and she remembered the time and felt bad. She went into the living-room, set her case down next to an armchair and threw her jacket on to the sofa. There was a note on the phone in Richard's writing saying that Caroline had called. No message. The day after Avendon was taken from Hamiltons with his heart episode, Caroline had called and in a very tiny and apologetic voice told her that she had decided to go back to Gareth. They were going to work things out properly. Karen had listened, making sounds that were neither negative nor positive. Caroline was not going back to Hamiltons either, another job for her to bail out of midway through. At college she and Caroline used to say all men *were* bastards, but some women were stupid. She stood and wondered whether she should call her. It was not her place to get in the middle of Caroline and Gareth, she thought.

'Hi honey, I'm home,' she called in her best American soap opera voice, hoping Richard was not going to be upset about the time. He was not in the kitchen, so she went to the bedroom where he lay on top of her bed, reading a fashion magazine.

'You're late,' he said to her, his eyes downcast and voice quieter than normal. She chose to ignore it.

'Big day tomorrow,' she replied, sitting down at her teak dressing table and removing her earrings. She was holding up well, but could detect the tiredness in her eyes that had been creeping up on her. She watched him in the mirror.

'Could have been a big night as well.' His tone was petulant.

'It's only ten-forty. Night's not over until the sun

comes up,' she said in a dirty voice.

'Whatever,' he mumbled, discarding the magazine and sitting up on the edge of the bed.

'When did Caroline call?'

'Just after seven. When I arrived.' He placed great emphasis on every word of the last sentence, as though speaking in capital letters to make a point.

She turned to face him. 'Richard, for Christ's sake, The Garden opens tomorrow. I can't just call time and walk out. What about when you do late Thursdays?'

'I wanted to do something special.'

The conversation was getting far too domestic for Karen.

'I only loaned you a set of keys, Richard, so you could let yourself in here tonight, remember? So you could *wait* for me? I made that clear. Please don't pull this wounded shit right now.'

'It's not about the keys or you being late,' he said to her.

'Exactly,' she responded.

'Are you seeing other people?'

She laughed. 'Of course I am. You know I am. I know you do as well. You'd better give me those keys back if they're going to make your balls this big all the time.'

'Who are you seeing?'

'Uh-uh.' She made the sound of a buzzer. 'Against the rules, remember?'

'I don't like the rules any more,' Richard said, looking away.

'So leave the game,' she came back instantly. Her words were even and the volume precise, neither too loud or too low.

He looked at her. 'Do you mean that?'

'I mean you should do what is best for you. We said all along that we were not going to get complicated. This is complicated, isn't it?'

'Whatever.'

She gave an exasperated sigh. '*Whatever*. Can't we

just re-run this scene? I come in, say hi, we ask how our days went and you give me a good hard seeing-to? Wouldn't that do, at least for tonight?'

Without a word, he grabbed her and threw her on to the bed. She said nothing and did nothing, allowing him to fling her harshly. He stuck his hands up under her skirt and ripped her underwear off, frantically pulling it over her shoes and then when he had done so, pulling her shoes off and throwing them so they fell loudly. His eyes burned like angry embers as he roughly undid and removed her skirt and stockings, fumbling frenziedly with her suspender belt. He put his hands to the collar of her blouse, where it was open, and gripped it. In one strong downward movement he ripped the buttons and in a second her top was off. He pulled her bra straps down over her shoulders and forced the whole thing off her breasts before he snapped away at the clasps behind her back.

Karen lay naked on the bed, the air inexplicably cold around her, having been crudely stripped in less than a minute. Her nudity was exciting to her under his angry gaze as he stood at the end of the bed and undid the belt on his trousers, zipping down the fly and popping the button at the top. He let them gape open and pushed the front of his briefs under his balls, allowing his cock to protrude. She opened her legs discreetly, making an area on the bed for him.

Richard gripped his cock and jerked it several times, his whole body making the required movements, and then he mounted the end of the bed. He advanced on her slowly, his cock hanging from him and pointing directly at her pussy. As he neared her, he supported himself on his left hand and his right held his cock, foreskin pulled far back. She braced herself.

'Is this what you fucking want? Is it?' he shouted at her, as if trying to be heard over noise.

She seethed as his cock pushed at her pussy-lips and entered her vagina. Her pussy was just slick enough to let him in, but the speed and the suddenness of it were still a shock to her system.

'Is this what you want?' His mouth was right by her ear and his breath was hot against it, spittle falling from his mouth on to her neck. 'A good hard seeing-to? Is it?'

'Yes,' she whimpered.

He pumped harder at her, his groin banging hers with a force that was audible.

'Is this hard enough?' he asked.

'You bastard,' she said to him, half pushing him away from her with her hands but her legs pulling on his hips to keep him inside of her. She dug her nails into the back of his shirt, pushing in as deeply as she could and he growled at her as she did.

'You bitch,' he snarled.

His cock was solid as it thrust at her. It was an intruder and did not feel a part of her in the same way it did when they normally made love. It was there serving only its own purpose and his own ends and there was a sadistic selfishness in his movements, seeking only to pleasure himself and to take that pleasure as quickly as possible. His drive into her was frenetic as though he were about to spill into her at any moment. He made grunting noises that were almost sobs as he fucked her hard and then harder still and she too cried out.

'Oh. Oh,' he moaned.

When he was about to come, she felt his cock actually swell in her pussy as his balls forced the first spurt of his come along his shaft. His face was a sneer as he grimaced at her and then fell into her, his full weight on her as his body jerked and snatched on her, his semen emptying from him into her. It was as intense an orgasm as she had ever seen him have and she gripped him tightly as he continued to come.

As quickly as he had stripped her and entered her, so he was gone from her. He pulled out roughly and stood up, his cock already going limp, some of his come on its tip and the shaft veneered with a film of her juices. He looked at her as he put himself back into his briefs and did up the button on his trousers. He was still angry, even after his orgasm, and it scared her. He pulled impatiently at his belt, looking as though he was pulling it tighter than he really needed to.

Standing at the end of the bed, he paused for a few seconds and Karen realised that he was waiting for her to say something, probably feeling he was giving her a chance. She said nothing, letting a long breath escape silently from her. He seemed to nod slightly as though acknowledging that there was nothing to say and he turned and walked out of the room.

Karen remained still on the bed, angry at him, at herself and at the whole situation. She sat up ready to speak, just in time to hear the sound of the front door being firmly slammed as he left.

'Richard!' she called out, but it was too late.

Chapter Nineteen

THERE WERE OVER two hundred people swarming around The Garden at the opening party and Karen loved it. Everything had run according to plan – as far as The Garden was concerned.

The last touches were still being put by two of the shop-fitters at four that afternoon, but they were now long gone, as was the balloon lady, the people delivering the food and drink and the people setting everything up. What remained were over twenty extremely cute waiters, an amazing spread of vegetarian food, the invited guests, the staff of The Garden and the press. People mingled with each other, snubbed each other, tried to pick each other up and got progressively more drunk on Hamiltons branded champagne. That side of things was absolutely fine.

On the other, things were very much not fine. Not at all. Richard had not been in Hamiltons that day and was not answering his phone at home. She had never seen him so upset and wondered where he was. He had promised to be her date at the party ages ago. When she called Caroline to invite her, the night before, Gareth had answered and she had just put the phone down, not wanting to get involved. Avendon was rumoured to be attending, but there was no sign of him yet and likewise with Linda and Maxwell. Chris Nichol had arrived with a model and was off somewhere, Karen not having had a chance to talk to him yet. David had temporarily disappeared. In short, she was in the middle of a large party for which she was mainly responsible and she suddenly felt very alone.

David appeared from nowhere and she made a line for him, practically grabbing at him when she reached him.

'Where have you been hiding?' she asked him, trying not to sound like his boss.

'I was showing Graham where we work,' he replied, moving aside so she could see Graham, the first man she had thought was right for The Garden. He was not, she noticed, wearing his fake horn-rims.

'Hi,' Graham said nonchalantly. 'Great party, Karen. David's been showing me your offices.'

'I can see that, Graham. Maybe you could tell him to do up his flies again,' she said as though David were not even there, looking down at his trousers as she spoke.

Graham gave a wicked laugh that subsided into a smile.

'Are you looking forward to working in The Garden?' Karen asked him.

'Of course I am. What else would I say?'

'True,' she replied. 'Cheer up, David; it's a party. We've done it.'

David seemed lost without his clipboard and nibbled on a nail to compensate for it.

'I think there should have been more balloons,' he said to Karen.

Karen laughed at him and was about to say something else when out of the corner of her eye she saw a whole set of flash guns go off at the same time. Maxwell. She turned, and there he was in the doorway with Linda, smiling politely as the photographers shouted at him to get his attention. The street entrance to Hamiltons was staked out by paparazzi and the rather large number of papers they had not invited. As she watched him, so polite and gentle, she wondered if

Linda had told him to be on his best behaviour. After a few more poses, they moved on and were quickly forgotten by the snap-happy bunch at the door. Karen excused herself from Graham and David, who had fallen into conversation and barely seemed to notice her, and went to greet Linda.

'Hello darling,' she said to Linda, who was clad in a smarter version of her normal black.

'You look great,' Linda said.

'Thank you,' said Karen, knowing she was right.

In a fit of indulgence, Karen had chosen the most outrageously expensive sequinned dress by Versace that she could find and she had arranged for her hairdresser to come into the store that afternoon and fix her hair before the party. The light caught the gold scales of the dress and accentuated her skin tone perfectly. She felt like a million dollars, which was handy because that was almost what her outfit had cost.

'Hi Karen,' Maxwell said, a spindly hand extending, his eyes on hers, thoughts on his mind, or so it seemed.

'Hello,' she pulled him to her with the hand and kissed him on the cheek, holding him for a fraction longer than she should have and several hours less than she would have liked.

'The picture on the dome looks good,' Linda said. 'It was worth all the effort.'

'Very Sistine Chapel, everyone says,' Karen told her.

Linda frowned. 'Caravaggio, maybe, but Michelangelo?' She raised her eyebrows. She looked around her, taking in The Garden.

'What do you think?' Karen asked her.

'I'd come here and shop. I will come here and shop. It's gorgeous, really. Look after Max, will you? I'm off to the bathroom.'

It was the first time she had spoken to Maxwell since that afternoon when they had been to Hyde Park and ended up back in her flat. Karen had spoken to Linda

201

several times, but not to Maxwell. He was dressed in a jacket with matching shorts that made him look like a schoolboy. His hair was better kept than normal and it seemed a shade darker than when she had seen him last. A small ache for him started somewhere in her chest.

'How have you been?' she asked him, cringing at the formality of the question.

'Centre of attention as usual,' he said resignedly. 'I was going to call you. I wish I had. I've thought about you quite a lot. You and Linda are very similar, but I don't think I'd be able to handle two at once.'

'You and Linda look very good together,' she said, feeling like Humphrey Bogart at the end of *Casablanca*, telling Ingrid Bergman to get on the plane with Victor Laszlo.

'You know what I'm saying, don't you?' he persisted.

'Max, Linda is one of my oldest friends and I hope you're going to be one of my newer ones. Let's not fuck things up with fucking. Agreed?'

'Even the toilets are sensational,' Linda said, returning, as Karen and Maxwell held each other's eyes and then broke.

'I know. Aren't they a scream?'

'Are there toilets for men?' Maxwell asked.

'Not in here. You have to go down on the lift and use the customer ones on the next floor down.'

He tutted and walked off in a minor huff, Karen and Linda watching him go.

'I'm mad about him,' Linda said to her.

'So am I,' she said, nudging her friend. 'I'll have him on the rebound.'

'He's still got a crush on you, Karen, you know don't you?'

'He was telling me that while you were in the loo.'

'What a sweetheart. Where's your beau, by the way?'

Karen looked at her and shook her head sadly.

'Trauma time, I'm afraid. He's not coming and anyway, he would have been my date, not my beau.'

'Point taken. Next subject.'

'What are you working on at the moment?' Karen asked.

'I'm finishing up on a book and then I've got about twenty commercial assignments to do. After that, I might do a whole book of Maxwell and birds. Are you going to oversee all of this gracefully?' Linda said, gesturing to The Garden.

'You know, I really don't know, Linda. This took up so much of my time, we haven't even thought about any other promotions, especially since Daniel's been away.'

'Is he going to be okay?'

'As far as we know. He's meant to be here tonight.'

'That's the boy from that stupid film with the car, isn't it?' Linda asked.

'Chris Nichol. Sexy, don't you think?'

'He certainly is,' Linda said. 'Too sexy to be with that giraffe.'

'Linda!'

'He's eyeing you, Karen. Look, he's coming over.' Linda was talking under her breath, the party ventriloquist skills long-established.

'Karen, hi,' Chris said, hugging her. 'This is Kit,' he continued, introducing the giraffe.

'This is my friend Linda Cole. She took the photographs you saw in the entrance. Ah, and here's the man himself,' Karen said as Maxwell returned.

'Maxwell, my baby!' said Kit in a fake East European voice and Linda made a face at Karen as the two of them hugged like they were being reunited after twenty years.

'Why don't we go and get some food,' Linda said, breaking into the Kit and Maxwell hug and leading them away. 'You remember food, don't you, Max? You had some once, I remember. Kit, you'll love the vine leaves. Very you . . .'

Linda's voice trailed off as she led the two of them away like they were her children, shrewdly leaving Chris and Karen alone.

'Did you come over specially for the party?' Karen asked him.

'I'd be lying if I said yes. I'm shooting a movie here.'

'Really? You never said.'

'It was last minute. I'm taking over from someone who's, shall we say, having trouble getting to the set each day.' He sniffed loudly and widened his eyes, acting as if off-balance from the effect of drugs.

'How long will you be here for?'

'Eight weeks,' he said.

'Have you seen much of Jake?'

Chris did the famous smile. 'He's on my back all the time. When will I do the movie. It's so right for me. It's the big crossover picture. All that stuff. Will we be able to spend some time together? While I'm here?'

She looked at him, a sigh about to break from her. First Maxwell and now Chris Nichol.

'Let's take it as it comes. Is that okay?' she asked tentatively.

'It's a start, I guess,' he smiled, no disappointment evident.

Linda returned alone.

'I've left them discussing the fat content of everything on the table. They'll be hours.' Linda grinned. 'I've photographed Kit for a shoe advert, before she was mega-famous. She's grown up a lot.'

'I love the pictures with the birds,' Chris said to Linda. 'It must have been hard to shoot.'

'It took a while, but we got there. I'd say I loved your last movie, but I hardly ever go,' Linda said baldly.

There was another minor commotion at the door, similar to when Linda and Maxwell had arrived. The three of them looked around and it was Daniel Avendon, smiling broadly and looking better than Karen could remember seeing him for a long while. She stared at him, almost shocked from not having seen him for so long and in her concentration she completely ignored who was hanging from his arm in a splendid ball-gown.

'Oh my god,' Linda was saying, tugging her arm, 'it's drippy Caroline with him!'

Karen's fixation on Avendon was broken and she stared at Caroline. Mousy Caroline. Holding Avendon's arm and smiling for the photographers as if she had been doing it all her life.

'When did she become Kate Moss?' Linda whispered to her.

'I have to go and talk to her,' Karen said, launching off across the room.

Caroline spotted Karen coming towards her and she broke away from Avendon, meeting her halfway.

'Hi,' Caroline said, bright and breezy.

'Hi? Caroline, what's going on?'

'I know. I'm sorry. I should have told you. It was easier to say I'd gone back to Gareth at the time. I tried to call you last night.'

'You haven't been with Gareth at all?' she asked.

'No way. Gareth came to Hamiltons the day Daniel collapsed. He'd seen that piece on you and The Garden in the paper and his little brain actually figured out I might be staying with you. He came looking for you and got more than he bargained for. It was sad, Karen. He was weeping, begging me. I sent him packing.'

'Have you been with Daniel all this time?'

'I was there when it happened. I went with him in the ambulance, stayed at the hospital and went with him to his country retreat while he was recovering. It was only a mild episode.'

'Did you see Gabrielle there?' Karen asked.

'She came several times. Daniel needs to talk to you about that.'

'Why?'

'I promised I'd let him tell you.' Caroline smiled at her.

'Caroline, are you and Daniel. . .?' she let the words trail off.

Caroline nodded. There was a beat of silence and then they giggled and embraced.

'Was that Linda Cole you were talking to?' Caroline asked. 'I haven't seen her in years. Make sure you have a word with Daniel. I'm going to chat with Linda, even though she never liked me, and we'll play catch-up later.'

Daniel had already been monopolised by several of his regular hangers-on and Karen took the time to gather her thoughts. She wished Richard was there. Or Alan. Or even Maxwell or Chris Nichol for that matter. The alone feeling returned to her.

'Excellent. Very good.'

Daniel laid a strong hand on her shoulder and she turned and smiled at him. They hugged, Karen realising it was the first time she had ever hugged him.

'Thank you. For everything,' she said to him. And she meant it. She could not have realised it without him and his backing. She would still be standing in Alan's kitchen with an apple in her hand and an idea in her head if it wasn't for Daniel Avendon.

'How are you feeling?' she asked him. 'You look well.'

'I feel well. Extremely. Have I missed any developments?'

'I feel like I have,' she said, nodding towards Caroline across the crowded floor.

'Yes. I'll fill you in on that saga presently. We should have a talk first. Soon. Now, really.'

'Caroline said you wanted a word. Shall we go to your office?'

'I've a better idea,' he said, taking her hand.

Daniel led her to the bottom of the stairs that led up to the gantry, the one that they had agreed would give a splendid view of The Garden and of the water wall at the back. It was guarded by someone from Hamiltons security as they had decided to close it for the party for fear of a drunken supermodel taking a tumble from her platform shoes and ending up on the floor below. When Avendon approached, the man jumped smartly aside and they climbed quickly to the top, Avendon in front.

'You seem in better condition than I do,' she said when they were on the gantry.

'Mistress of all you see. All.' He looked at her and then at his watch.

'Are you all right?'

'Yes. Hate drama, though. They should be here any minute, so I should spill this one now.' He seemed to be talking to himself.

'Spill what?'

He looked at her and then concentrated on the throng below. Up on the walkway, they were hidden, the spotlights off and the gantry only dimly lit. They watched silently for a few moments. Then Daniel seemed to draw a very long breath, as if about to blow up a balloon, and he spoke.

'I thought we would be better up here. You can hear it from me that way. There is no really good way to tell it or make it sound sensible.'

They were three of the longest sentences Karen had ever heard Daniel Avendon utter and she was now intrigued.

'When Gabrielle left the shop in sixty-nine,' he continued, 'it was not to have a break. Far from it. She was pregnant. She carried the child to term and at birth it was adopted. Gabrielle named him after her father, Dick Foxton and gave him her mother's maiden name as his surname. That was how he came to be called Richard Fraser.'

Karen turned and stared hard at Avendon, Richard's name stabbing at her and sounding wrong in the context it was being used. That was how he came to be called Richard Fraser? Gabrielle was Richard's mother? She was about to say something, not even sure what, when Avendon cut her off by continuing to speak.

'Also, that gave the boy no connection to his father, Alan Saxton. The whole time was really very difficult. Indeed. For all involved. Alan was still married to Margaret at the time, and I still say they were right for each other, regardless of his dalliance with my half-sister. After the adoption, Gabrielle had no interest in the boy or in Alan. Her only interest was in keeping the two of them separated. It was ironic, really, because Alan looked after the trust fund we set up for him.'

Karen eyed him and Avendon laughed.

'Oh yes,' he said. 'He doesn't have to work. Never. Alan thought a bit of time in the trenches would serve him well before we drag him upstairs. As lovely as your friend Caroline is, I'm not in the market to sire an heir at my age. Richard will suffice. Ah, there we are, on perfect dramatic cue.'

They looked down and Gabrielle and Alan had arrived, Richard with them. Karen looked down on the scene, at a wonderful vantage point but lost for words.

'When Gabrielle found out he was working here, she felt that history, the history of our fathers at least, was about to be repeated in some manner. There was little trouble she could stir up for Alan at that point as he was divorced from Margaret and Richard knows his own mind. She had no ammunition and that's why she came after the shop, in a manner of speaking.'

Karen looked over the edge, the gantry seeming higher than it did only moments earlier, her perspective on the whole scene below shifting along with Avendon's words as they calmly reordered the world for her. The taunts Richard had made to her about Alan, the way Alan had talked about children and the photograph of the supposed nephew that he had explained away so badly when they were at his house in the country. She found some words.

'Why would she come for the shop? Wouldn't she want what was best for her son?' Karen asked him.

'Yes. Of course. She believes she is doing what is in

his best interests by being here. She lost someone very close to her last year and that seemed to spark this off in her. I think she felt alone and wanted to grab on to the past. Richard was the only bit available and he was linked with Hamiltons by then. Richard is the thing that binds the feud in many ways. The Avendons and the Foxtons, let alone the Saxtons.'

'What is she going to do?'

'She's trying to be mysterious, but I suspect she will transfer her holding to Richard. It will work itself out. The Garden will succeed, you know that, don't you?'

'Yes,' she replied.

'We may be relying on you heavily with this venture, I feel. And I feel confident. Extremely so. And I think they will succeed too,' he said, looking down at Gabrielle and Alan, talking intimately and seemingly drawn together by an invisible force that had been nurtured for over twenty years.

At first it was no more than a trickle and then it became a gentle flow and finally it was a cascade as water poured over the top of the grey marble water wall. The lights flashed on, illuminating the water and the gantry at the same time. All eyes in the room were upturned and after a minute or two, applause broke out. Avendon took Karen's hand and squeezed it, a grin on his face, and it was then that she realised the applause was for her. For a full minute she beamed radiantly and then searched the crowd below for the face she was looking for.

Finding it, and with her eyes fixed on his, she descended slowly into the applause.

Chapter Twenty

NEARLY TWO YEARS after the grand opening party that launched The Garden that Friday evening, both Daniel Avendon's words and the applause still rang in Karen Taylor's ears. And the applause went on in other ways. On reflection, many of the things that had happened at the party had laid the basis for what followed.

Now, she was taking a quiet moment, lying in bed having recently made love and about to look at a book. She reached over to her side-table, careful not to disturb the gently snoozing form beside her, and picked it up. Its title was very simple, much as Linda had said it would be when she had first mentioned it to Karen all that time ago. It was called 'Maxwell and Birds'. It had been very successful as photographic books went and she had an exhibition accompanying it at the Hayward Gallery. In their strange way, Linda and Maxwell were still an item. By capturing him so consistently and continually on film, Linda seemed to be turning the pair of them into something that extended far beyond being a couple. Karen wondered where they would go next. Linda's photography of him was stunning, many different poses and ideas, including Maxwell in cages and Maxwell wearing feathers and little else. The three pictures Linda had taken for Hamiltons to promote the fragrance and The Garden were also used, with a kind thank you extended to Daniel Avendon in the introduction.

Leafing through the pictures of him, she remembered her time with him and the times they had spent together since then, every once in a while. Karen was tired and drifting into sleep. She had a meeting in Paris the next day to talk about opening a branch of The Garden. It would be the fifth. Next year, she would move beyond Europe and look to establish branches in New York and Beverly Hills. In numerous interviews and profiles, they tried to get Karen to pin down the essence of The Garden and what had made it so successful. If she seemed elusive, it was because an answer very often eluded her. She knew she had tapped into something, done something right, and she was not about to pick it to pieces while it was still working.

Setting up the first independent branch of The Garden in London had been Alan's idea. It was still associated with Hamiltons, but the separation gave her much more scope to expand both in terms of size and with some of the other concepts that had suggested themselves. As with the original Garden, Alan had been extremely supportive and helpful. The first month or so after The Garden opened at Hamiltons had been a difficult period for Karen and Alan. They felt awkward with each other, both knowing that they should have told their secrets to each other sooner. To his credit, he had seemed quite amused when he found out that she had also been seeing his son behind his back. More amused, in truth, than when Karen had discovered that Richard was Alan's son.

During that difficult period, Chris Nichol had been a source of great solace to her. They started out by jumping on each other the moment they met but by the time he went back to the States, they spent more time talking than having sex. Chris still phoned her from time to time to make sure she was all right and she would call him to do likewise, normally because she had read some piece of untrue gossip about him.

She was glad to have him as a friend.

Karen lay and wondered if her flight had been properly booked this time. She missed David. Graham had published a minor blockbuster based on his catwalk days that had been optioned for a vast sum of money by a production company in Hollywood, and he had whisked David off with him. He sent her the occasional postcard, the words still full of wonder at being out in Los Angeles as Graham's 'personal assistant'. An image of David and clipboard formed in her mind and she smiled to herself.

Karen also missed Hamiltons, but she knew that The Garden chain was the way to go. Daniel had cut a very favourable deal for her and she had reaped the rewards quickly. Daniel's role at Hamiltons had become much more back-seat and Alan and Richard between them handled most of the business on a day-to-day basis, Daniel becoming increasingly royal and enjoying it immensely. Karen was amazed at the transformation in Richard, the way he had picked up the business so quickly and how sharp he was. Perhaps it was in the blood.

At that moment, Daniel and Alan were off on a cruise with Gabrielle and Caroline, doing whatever the four of them did in their fairly tight-knit social group. Karen marvelled at how four people like that could get on. Alan and Daniel were very alike, but it was hard to think of more different people than Caroline and Gabrielle. Karen was pleased for Caroline that she was still with Daniel. With Alan, she did not understand what he saw in Gabrielle, who had changed very little over the period Karen had known her. With Richard more involved in Hamiltons, Gabrielle had lost interest in the shop and The Garden, so her relationship with Richard and Alan had served its purpose from that point of view.

With the four of them off cruising, a lot of the responsibility for Hamiltons was left with Richard. He seemed to be handling it well, she thought, as she turned and looked at him sleeping, his face making the occasional gesture. She reached out and rubbed his shoulder. He murmured something and rolled towards her, putting an arm around her and squeezing, asleep the whole time.

Gently, she discarded Maxwell and the birds and switched off the lamp, enjoying the first few seconds of total darkness. All her thoughts and mental energy were slowly overtaken by pure feeling as she moved herself closer to him.

In the warmth of his body, she fell asleep.

BACK IN CHARGE
Mariah Greene

A woman in control. Sexy, successful, sure of herself and of what she wants, Andrea King is an ambitious account handler in a top advertising agency. Life seems sweet, as she heads for promotion and enjoys the attentions of her virile young boyfriend.

But strange things are afoot at the agency. A shake-up is ordered, with the key job of Creative Director in the balance. Andrea has her rivals for the post, but when the chance of winning a major new account presents itself, she will go to any lengths to please her client – and herself . . .

0 7515 1276 1

THE DISCIPLINE OF PEARLS
Susan Swann

A mysterious gift, handed to her by a dark and arrogant stranger. Who was he? How did he know so much about her? How did he know her life was crying out for something different? Something . . . exciting, erotic?

The pearl pendant, and the accompanying card bearing an unknown telephone number, propel Marika into a world of uninhibited sexuality, filled with the promise of a desire she had never thought possible. The Discipline of Pearls . . . an exclusive society that speaks to the very core of her sexual being, bringing with it calls to ecstasies she is powerless to ignore, unwilling to resist . . .

0 7515 1277 X

HOTEL APHRODISIA
Dorothy Starr

The luxury hotel of Bouvier Manor nestles near a spring whose mineral water is reputed to have powerful aphrodisiac qualities. Whether this is true or not, Dani Stratton, the hotel's feisty receptionist, finds concentrating on work rather tricky, particularly when the muscularly attractive Mitch is around.

And even as a mysterious consortium threatens to take over the Manor, staff and guests seem quite unable to control their insatiable thirsts . . .

0 7515 1287 7

AROUSING ANNA
Nina Sheridan

Anna had always assumed she was frigid. At least, that's what her husband Paul had always told her – in between telling her to keep still during their brief weekly fumblings under the covers and playing the field himself during his many business trips.

But one such trip provides the chance that Anna didn't even know she was yearning for. Agreeing to put up a lecturer who is visiting the university where she works, she expects to be host to a dry, elderly academic, and certainly isn't expecting a dashing young Frenchman who immediately speaks to her innermost desires. And, much to her delight and surprise, the vibrant Dominic proves himself able and willing to apply himself to the task of arousing Anna . . .

0 7515 1222 2

THE WOMEN'S CLUB
Vanessa Davies

Sybarites is a health club with a difference. Its owner, Julia Marquis, has introduced a full range of services to guarantee complete satisfaction. For after their saunas and facials the exclusively female members can enjoy an 'intimate' massage from one of the club's expert masseurs.

And now, with the arrival of Grant Delaney, it seems the privileged clientele of the women's club will be getting even better value for their money. This talented masseur can fulfil any woman's erotic dreams.

Except Julia's . . .

0 7515 1343 1

PLAYING THE GAME
Selina Seymour

Kate has had enough. No longer is she prepared to pander to the whims of lovers who don't love her; no longer will she cater for their desires while neglecting her own.

But in reaching this decision Kate makes a startling discovery: the potency of her sexual urge, now given free rein through her willingness to play men at their own game. And it is an urge that doesn't go unnoticed – whether at her chauvinistic City firm, at the château of a new French client, or in performing the duties of a high-class call girl . . .

0 7515 1189 7

A SLAVE TO HIS KISS
Anastasia Dubois

When her twin sister Cassie goes missing in the South of France, Venetia Fellowes knows she must do everything in her power to find her. But in the dusty village of Valazur, where Cassie was last seen, a strange aura of complicity connects those who knew her, heightened by an atmosphere of unrestrained sexuality.

As her fears for Cassie's safety mount, Venetia turns to the one person who might be able to help: the enigmatic Esteban, a study in sexual mystery whose powerful spell demands the ultimate sacrifice . . .

0 7515 1344 X

SATURNALIA
Zara Devereux

Recently widowed, Heather Logan is concerned about her sex-life. Even when married it was plainly unsatisfactory, and now the prospects for sexual fulfilment look decidedly thin.

After consulting a worldly friend, however, Heather takes his advice and checks in to Tostavyn Grange, a private hotel-cum-therapy centre for sexual inhibition. Heather had been warned about their 'unconventional' methods, but after the preliminary session, in which she is brought to a thunderous climax – her first – she is more than willing to complete the course . . .

0 7515 1342 3

DARES
Roxanne Morgan

It began over lunch. Three different women, best friends, decide to spice up their love-lives with a little extra-curricular sex. Shannon is first, accepting the dare of seducing a motorcycle despatch rider – while riding pillion through the streets of London.

The others follow, Nadia and Corey, hesitant at first but soon willing to risk all in the pursuit of new experiences and the heady thrill of trying to out-do each other's increasingly outrageous dares . . .

0 7515 1341 5

Forthcoming publications

INSPIRATION
Stephanie Ash

They were both talented painters, but three years of struggling to make a living from art have rather taken the edge off Clare's relationship with her boyfriend. The temptation to add a few more colours to her palette seems increasingly attractive – and proves irresistible when she meets the enigmatic and charming Steve.

But their affair is complicated when Steve's beautiful wife asks Clare to paint his portrait as a birthday surprise. Clare is more than happy to suffer for her art – indulging in some passionate studies of her model *and* her client – but when a jealous friend gets involved the situation calls for more intimate inspiration . . .

0 7515 1489 6

DARK SECRET
Marina Anderson

Harriet Radcliffe was bored with her life. At twenty-three, her steady job and safe engagement suddenly seemed very dull. If she was to inject a little excitement into her life, she realised, now was the time to do it.

But the excitement that lay in store was beyond even her wildest ambitions. Answering a job advertisement to assist a world-famous actress, Harriet finds herself plunged into an intense, enclosed world of sexual obsession – playing an unwitting part in a very private drama, but discovering in the process more about her own desires than she had ever dreamed possible . . .

0 7515 1490 X

[ ]	Back in Charge	Mariah Greene	£4.99
[ ]	The Discipline of Pearls	Susan Swann	£4.99
[ ]	Hotel Aphrodisia	Dorothy Starr	£4.99
[ ]	Arousing Anna	Nina Sheridan	£4.99
[ ]	Playing the Game	Selina Seymour	£4.99
[ ]	The Women's Club	Vanessa Davies	£4.99
[ ]	A Slave to His Kiss	Anastasia Dubois	£4.99
[ ]	Saturnalia	Zara Devereux	£4.99
[ ]	Dares	Roxanne Morgan	£4.99

X Libris offers an eXciting range of quality titles which can be ordered from the following address:

Little, Brown and Company (UK),
P.O. Box 11,
Falmouth,
Cornwall TR10 9EN

Alternatively you may fax your order to the above address.
FAX No. 0326 376423.

Payments can be made as follows: cheque, postal order (payable to Little, Brown and Company) or by credit cards, Visa/Access. Do not send cash or currency. UK customers and B.F.P.O. please allow £1.00 for postage and packing for the first book, plus 50p for the second book, plus 30p for each additional book up to a maximum charge of £3.00 (7 books plus).

Overseas customers including Ireland please allow £2.00 for the first book plus £1.00 for the second book, plus 50p for each additional book.

NAME (Block Letters) _____

_____

ADDRESS _____

_____

_____

☐ I enclose my remittance for _____

☐ I wish to pay by Access/Visa card

Number _____

Card Expiry Date _____